REA

366-

1900.

A priest's diary

Diary

A Priest's Diary

by

Sigbjørn Obstfelder

Translated and with an introduction by
James McFarlane

Norvik Press
1987

Published titles:
Michael Robinson: *Strindberg and Autobiography*

Forthcoming titles:
Bjørg Vik: *An Aquarium of Women,* translated by Janet Garton
Hjalmar Söderberg: *Selected Short Stories* translated by Carl Lofmark
Annegret Heitmann (ed.): *No Man's Land* – an anthology of Danish women writers
Irene Scobbie (ed.): *Studies in Modern Swedish Literature*

Our logo is based on a drawing by Egil Bakka (University of Bergen) of a Viking ornament in gold foil, paper thin, with impressed figures (size 16 x 21 mm). It was found in 1897 at Hauge, Klepp, Rogaland, and is now in the collection of the Historisk museum, University of Bergen (inv.no.5392). It depicts a love scene, possibly (according to Magnus Olsen) between the fertility god Freyr and the maiden Gerðr; the large penannular brooch of the man's cloak dates the work as being most likely 10th century.

The portrait of Obstfelder is a lithograph by Edvard Munch.

(*En prests dagbog* was first published in 1900, and reprinted as part of Sigbjørn Obstfelder: *Samlede Skrifter* in 3 volumes, edited by Solveig Tunold, published by Gyldendal Norsk Forlag, Oslo, 1950.)

© 1987 by James McFarlane
All Rights Reserved
ISBN 1-870041-01-1

First published in 1987 by Norvik Press, University of East Anglia, Norwich, NR4 7TJ.

Managing Editors: James McFarlane and Janet Garton

Norvik Press has been established with financial support from the University of East Anglia, the Danish Ministry for Cultural Affairs, the Norwegian Cultural Department, the Norwegian Cultural Council, and the Swedish Institute.

Publication of this book has been aided by a grant from the Norwegian Cultural Council.
Printed in Great Britain by the University of East Anglia, Norwich.

CONTENTS

CONTENTS

PREFACE

My attention was first drawn to Obstfelder more than thirty years ago by Solveig Tunold, editor of the three volume edition of Obstfelder's collected works and the then head of the Manuscript Department of Oslo University Library. I shall always be grateful to her not only for that introduction but also for the kindness she showed me during the many years I consulted those manuscript collections over which she presided with such quiet erudition and loving care.

More recently I have had cause to be grateful to Arne Hannevik, of the Institute for Literary Theory and Criticism in the University of Oslo, editor of Obstfelder's letters and author of *Obstfelder og mystikken* (Oslo, 1960), for help and enlightenment on a number of specific points of detail, and particularly in regard to the draft fragments of the book's continuation. I also owe a debt of gratitude to my colleague in the University of East Anglia, Janet Garton, for her unfailingly helpful comments and advice. My best thanks go to them both.

The economics of book publishing do not easily permit one to follow Obstfelder's own declared wishes on the matter of the make-up of the printed page of this book. The individual sections are marked off from each other in his own fair-copy manuscript fragment with a '*', which is the convention used in this book. In a letter of 27 July 1899 to Tyra Bentsen which accompanied this manuscript fragment, Obstfelder wrote: 'As you see, I have divided the book up into small sections. Where a section ends, the remainder of the page should be left blank. And the next section should begin some way down the following page - more than I have indicated.'

Finally, I have to confess to a measure of self-plagiarism in that certain passages in the following Introduction first appeared in the chapter on Obstfelder in my book *Ibsen and the Temper of Norwegian Literature* (London: Oxford University Press, 1960).

JWMcF
October 1986

INTRODUCTION

The turn of the century was confident that it knew where authentic religious experience was most reliably recorded, most accessibly defined. Not in the findings of academic theology or biblical scholarship, not in what William James dismissively called the 'abstract definitions and systems of logically concatenated adjectives' of these and similar secondary accretions upon religion, but rather in the testimony of private, humble minds, in the accounts of those concrete religious experiences at the level of feeling and conduct which renew themselves *in saecula saeculorum* in the lives of certain diffident and bewildered and anguished individuals.

What then, in the opinion of the age, was the characteristic nature of such experiences? James himself - whose Gifford Lectures of 1901-02 at the University of Edinburgh on the nature of Natural Religion (later published under the better-known title of *The Varieties of Religious Experience*) constitute one of the great classic pronouncements on these and related matters - ventured a brief catalogue:

> ...They are conversations with the unseen, voices and visions, responses to prayer, changes of heart, deliverances from fear, inflowings of help, assurances of support, whenever certain persons set their own internal attitude in certain appropriate ways.

His phrases resonate strongly with Sigbjørn Obstfelder's *A Priest's Diary*. Almost as though in obedience to these Jamesian promptings, Sigbjørn Obstfelder set his own 'internal attitude', set it in his own highly distinctive and idiosyncratic way, and after some years of anguished self-interrogation, began the composition of what he clearly intended should be his major work. Alas, the work was destined to remain unfinished. It survives now as a fragment: the initial section of a work seemingly planned on a greatly ambitious scale but cruelly cut short by sickness and ultimately by the author's death in 1900.

Sigbjørn Obstfelder and his work are totally and uniquely of the Eighteen Nineties. As few others, he was attuned to the epoch into which he was born, in touch with its secret springs, aligned with its changing directions. Born on 21 November 1866 as the seventh of sixteen children, compelled in 1891 to enter a mental asylum for some months to regain the balance of his mind, Obstfelder died of consumption at the age of thirty-three on 29 July 1900, the same year that witnessed the untimely deaths of those other representative figures of the age: Oscar Wilde and Ernest Dowson. It is almost as though his soul, like theirs, could not endure the passing of the decade. Yet for all the sadness and the sense of unfulfilled promise attaching to his early death, there was nevertheless something grimly appropriate about the timing and the manner of it, as though by by his dying he was seeking to add one final and almost ostentatious proof that his soul was ineluctably linked with the spirit of the *fin-de-siècle*. Even the last and characteristically macabre touch was not lacking; for on the same day that he was carried to his grave, his widow was delivered of their only child. It is with good reason that more than one contemporary author - among their number Rilke - have been suspected of using Obstfelder as a model on which to create some fictional character typical of the age.

His first volume of poems was published in 1893; *A Priest's Diary* - his last work - appeared posthumously in 1900. To the years between there belongs a quantitatively modest but highly distinctive *oeuvre*: a number of plays and dramatic fragments, including *The Red Drops* (1897) and two one-act plays *In Spring* (1898) and *Esther* (1899), several short prose works, among them the short stories *The Cross* (1895) and *The Plain* (1895), and a large number of fugitive pieces, sketches, articles, drafts and reminiscences, together with a group of works which he called 'poems in prose'.

Literary scholarship recognises in the name of Obstfelder that of the young man on whom Rilke is believed to have modelled the diarist hero of *Die Aufzeichnungen des Malte Laurids Brigge*. It is known that Rilke was acquainted with Obstfelder's work before he began work on *Malte*; his correspondence of these years contains occasional mention of the Norwegian poet by name, and on 4 December 1904 he sent as a gift to Lou Andreas-Salomé a book by Obstfelder - it is uncertain which - with the comment: 'Ein kleines Buch von Obstfelder sende ich dir, darin das und jenes mir lieb geworden ist.' On another occasion he described Obstfelder as 'a poet of subtle impressionism and intense sensibility'. Most probably however it was the man, his personality and his fate - details of which Rilke may well have learned of from Ellen Key, at different times the confidante of both men - rather than the works themselves that provided Rilke with a starting point for *Malte*. As Rilke was later to tell Maurice Betz, his French translator, there were two very obvious points of convergence: Obstfelder, like the fictional Malte, had lived as a Scandinavian in Paris; and he was also very characteristic of those gifted *Früheentrückten* who die young without having been able to give to their work the full measure of their tormented and generous souls. Obstfelder might then - as one perspicacious critic has suggested - be seen standing to Malte as Jerusalem stood to Goethe's Werther: 'The suicide of Jerusalem, and the death of the young Norwegian Sigbjørn Obstfelder, provided the two high priests of poetry with the . . . victim, whose blood had to drench the altar.'

The torment of soul which Rilke remarked in Obstfelder is conspicuous as the most characteristic feature of his life and work. Yet it coloured his poetry and determined his life not so much by the nature of the elements of which it was compounded, nor even by the intensity with which it manifested itself, as by his own anguished awareness of and insight into it. Above all he was racked by the problems of how to reconcile one's worth as a solitary, independent and creative spirit, questioning, brooding, uncertain, with one's responsibilities to society and to one's fellows and of how to meet the need for confident and purposeful action. 'It is only when one sees the great cities, the beating hearts of the age,' he wrote in 1894, 'that one experiences the urge to feel oneself *at one* with this working, suffering, and sinning society of men, to understand what it does and what it leaves undone, to share sickness with the sick, and to understand that one might be able to heal.' Mystical by nature, materialistic by conscience, he found obsessive the problem of how to hold the balance. The tenacity with which he carried through decisions once they had been taken was stiffened by the knowledge of his own paralyzing irresolution: 'Moodiness [*tungsindet*] -this word which I have pronounced so many times - undermines me and my will. And when it is not moodiness, then it is irresolution. I set myself objectives, I draw up lists in my tormented brain, but all that happens is that not a single heading on my lists is ever accomplished - as the result of my sinking into brooding about it.' His letters bear witness to the variety of plans he toyed with and the rapidity with which he switched from one scheme to another - one of which, incidentally, was to learn English well enough to become a worthy successor to Walt Whitman. But always the main tension with him - as it was also to be with his priestly diarist -was that between what lies within the individual and what exists without, between solitary contemplation and social action. By his determination to immerse himself in life, to discipline within himself what could be disciplined only at fearful cost, he kept at high tension the torment in his mind and soul, driving himself to the point where his reason temporarily collapsed and ultimately perhaps to his death.

A rough graph of his life's history shows the violence of the fluctuations to which this inner conflict subjected him. As an introspective child he had given evidence of considerable imaginative gifts; and when he was of an age to enter university, he enrolled as a student of philology, leaving himself free also to pursue his interests in music, literature and philosophy. (It is no surprise, in the light of certain passages in *A Priest's Diary*, to discover that Kierkegaard occupied him greatly at this time.) But then in 1888 came one of those decisions that social conscience and an inner compulsion to contribute to the material good of society combined to urge upon him: he abandoned his humanistic studies in favour of engineering. After two years of study at a technical college, he emigrated to America to join his younger brother in the late summer of 1890. But his life there - first in Milwaukee, later in Washington Heights and Chicago - was one of disappointment and frustration. Before long the deeper forces in his nature began once more to assert themselves; and he determined to return home to Europe, to turn his back on engineering, and to devote himself to that art which is perhaps at the furthest remove from materialism: music. Arriving back in Norway in 1891, weary and dispirited, he almost at once suffered mental collapse. Later the old conflicts merely took new form; he embarked on a literary career, but alongside his poetry he felt the compulsion to participate in the social debates of the age; he contributed many articles on the controversial questions of the day, on temperance, on the role of women in society, on modern architecture. His restless spirit drove him to lead a wandering, rootless existence which, as some of his letters show, was painfully at odds with his deep-seated desire to marry and settle down to a life of quiet purposeful endeavour. Copenhagen and Paris, Stockholm and Berlin, Amsterdam, Prague and London saw him for brief periods. Eventually he did marry, but his dreams of contentment and quiet fulfilment were not realised, and his death followed only two years later.

What marks him off from most of his European contemporaries in art and literature is the degree of self-discipline he sought to impose upon himself in an age in which self-indulgence and self-abandonment were the more usual hallmarks of the artistic temperament. Where others might take pride in their greater sensitivity or the fine tuning of their aesthetic responses, he claimed distinction for himself rather for his efforts at self-control. Not sensitivity but strength of purpose was what, in his own estimation, gave distinction to his literary activities: few other young writers, he asserted, were possessed of the strength of will he himself had shown to hold fast to a composition over the years. Where others had seen their sensibility as a thing to be carefully tended and nurtured, he himself was only too conscious of the threat it posed to his achieving a wholly fulfilled life; where others had sought to escape from an oppressive reality into a world of vivid and possibly exotic sensation, he recognised the dangers of this for him and sought endlessly to resist. Despite a strong streak of eroticism in his make-up, he advocated and practised self-control in sexual matters: as early as 1887, writing on the question of sexual restraint among young men, he claimed with some satisfaction that he was 'one of the few who have really striven to be worthy of Woman in this respect'. There was no easy thrill for him in abandoning oneself to the ecstasy of the moment, but rather a sense of betrayal and guilt. There was nothing in him of the *poseur*, being too painfully aware of the dangers in what Walt Whitman had called 'the hiatus in singular eminence', a remoteness from common life. Engagement, not detachment, was pre-eminently what Obstfelder sought from life.

The percipience that was his, he therefore employed not as the means by which to experience ever more vivid and unusual sensation but rather as an instrument to aid him in his quest for meaning in the universe. 'I believe,' he wrote to a friend in 1895 (the year in which he began work on *A Priest's Diary*), 'that I have, as scarcely any other young author has, the urge to penetrate into the mystery of nature, to see Man in the light of what is eternal in time, space and energy, to see the changing forms of life, flower, larva, infusoria in great array as the song of Universal Life.' Poets, he says in one of his shorter articles, are like those who lend us lenses, telescopes, microscopes, the better to see and comprehend what is all around us. Sensibility is not the stuff of self-indulgence; it is a working instrument, a device for attempting to trace and record the connections between things, connections too tenuous and too fine for the commonplace mind to capture.

All this is clearly mirrored in *A Priest's Diary*. Rilke's reported summary of it - 'the story of a soul who, in his despairing attempts to reach God, actually becomes more estranged from Him, a prey to an intellectual fever that brings him to despair' - is true only in part. (One cannot actually be sure that Rilke's comments were based on first-hand reading of the work, or indeed whether he was correctly reported.) Much of the book, it is true, grew out of the mental turmoil of his earlier breakdown - it is not without significance that Obstfelder requested that certain of his letters written to his brother from the asylum should be returned to him. It is also the case that Obstfelder more and more came to see the problems of existence as religious problems. But the mysticism is only one aspect, just as the problems of practical living are another, of something much more comprehensive, more diffuse: the purpose of life itself, the search for some kind of certainty in a deeply uncertain world, whether that certainty concerns the nature of God on the one hand or the imperatives of community living on the other. The bishop, the doctor and the worker all have, in this diary, their own kind of certainty, their own confident belief in some adopted faith: dogmatic, social, materialist, as the case may be. Only the lonely poet has doubts and the compulsion to express them. *A Priest's Diary* is a book with the courage of its lack of convictions.

The diary is that of one who, echoing James's phrases, is essentially a humble and devoutly private individual. The title of the work assigns the diarist to the priesthood, yet the particular constraints of priesthood figure at relatively few points in the account: there is reference to the anguish of conscience he suffers when officiating at holy communion, to the dread he feels at confronting his saintly bishop and his fellow priests, and (in the manuscript fragment which continues the diary beyond the end of the published text) to the peculiar sense of incongruity which assails him when, as a priest, he enters the heavily sensual atmosphere of the cheap dance hall. But, as Ibsen had once claimed in respect of his priestly protagonist Brand, this was not a particularly material factor: Brand, said Ibsen, might just as well have been a sculptor or a poet. The defining characteristic of the priest whose diary this purports to be is simply that his personal response to the challenge of contemporary life is of such importunate sensitivity that he is driven tirelessly to explore the quotidian mysteries of life, to record both them and his own responses to them with the kind of painfully scrupulous honesty which will (he trusts) carry him along to greater clarity and insight.

The priestly diarist is a man sustained by a conviction that within the cluttered and chaotic and often menacing immediacy of life there lies some coherent, reductive, ordering principle waiting to be laid bare. He is driven to move through his world, to expose himself to it, even though he knows he will emerge wounded and lacerated from the ordeal. He reaches out to seize hold of life, holds it up for meticulous examination and anguished scrutiny, interrogates every experience and every sense impression, querying its purpose, baring its antecedents, plotting its destination and goal. Sorely vulnerable yet at the same time strangely inviolate, he obeys this inner imperative to experience all - the beauty, the terror, the ecstasy, the repulsiveness, the mystery - sorely vulnerable and yet at the same time strangely inviolate, all the while doggedly recording his own responses in the style of William James's 'humble private man'.

His dementia is for things too elusive to be caught by merely cerebral explanation, for things beyond the conventional power of words. In the pages of his diary, the priest drives impatiently on from the rational and the sensory to the extra-sensory in the hope that ultimately some kind of intuitive empathy will throw light on life's profounder secrets. For him the contemporary world is in ceaseless and mostly reciprocal motion: tremulous, vibrant, quivering. Nature is less a thing of substance than a complex organism of rhythms and frequencies: the changing play of light, the inhalation and exhalation of beasts and plants, the endless aspirations, respirations and palpitations of life's processes. Stability, repose and a sense of unchanging permanence he finds only in past ages, beyond recall except through the intermediacy of nostalgia. Where once there were absolutes, he now finds only relativities. What once seemed whole and solid is now a pattern of insubstantiality, a febrile atomic dance.

Obstfelder himself was very ready to admit that his text lacked narrative progression, any sustained continuity. The diarist's mode of existence is contemplative; his perceived role that of universal observer. 'Reality' for him was pluralist: the din of the locomotive sheds; the flattened bed-bug on the sheets; the rat scuttling across the floor. But equally it was the solicitude of his benign white-haired old bishop, the confident idealism of the materialistic doctor, the purposeful and single-minded industry of all those who contributed to society by their labour. There is no commitment on his part to any form of decisive action, greatly though he yearns for the opportunity. The most he actually does is *go* somewhere: on to the streets, into the factory, to the concert hall, to the mountain top. He hoards his sensations, stockpiles his perceptions, brooding over them as over some priceless treasure of *objets trouvés*. Yet despite the disjunction, despite the essentially episodic nature of his report on his experiences, the parts nevertheless cohere, held together by the intensity of his quest for meaning.

Some have seen in Obstfelder's work an attempt to do in language what his great contemporary Edvard Munch was currently doing in paint. Obstfelder's own assessment of Munch may indeed have greater validity as unconscious *self*-criticism than it does as objective comment. Arguing that Munch was a *receptive* artist whose greatness lay more in the subtlety of his colour than in his power to reshape or manipulate the observed and received forms of life, and claiming that Munch's genius did not run to the creation of 'new lines', Obstfelder went on:

> But those lines that *are*, those he sees as no other man. And it is as if, from all that exists, from all existence with all its forms and all its chaos, he extracts *one* line which he constantly worked towards and which he endeavours to turn more and more beautifully. Is it the line of his inmost Self? Or is it the one drawn by the encounter between his soul's plan and that of the universe about him?

These phrases have an immediate relevance to *A Priest's Diary*. The line it pursues - and would have pursued further if time and health had permitted - is that traced by the encounter between Obstfelder's own tormented soul and cosmic reality. Obstfelder's strengths as a writer lay less in his ability to project his experiences, to give them a newly moulded form of poetic invention, than they did in his capacity to marvel, to stand and look and listen and dream and then to record. In this work he does not set out to create a poetic world complete with its own inner and inherent laws but instead endeavours, with the utmost delicacy, to follow the twists and turns, the evasions, the probings and the withdrawals of a soul's progress in its exploration of this world.

To call his work symbolist, as is often done, is thus true in only a very limited sense. Visionary is rather the term that more exactly describes his highly personal way of attempting to say the Unsayable -'those feelings,' as he wrote in his early student days, 'which have not acquired the form of thought'. Whereas Rilke for his part devised a range of symbols (the angel, the puppet, the acrobat, for example) to aid him in his attempts to say *das Unsägliche*, Obstfelder found that what he had similarly termed *det usigelige* communicated itself more particularly in visions. Time and again in *A Priest's Diary*, the sense of the mysterious Oneness that fills the universe is translated into essentially visual terms: patterns, networks, barely visible threads that link the things of life. Even music (which meant so much to him and for which he showed so sensitive an understanding) is a thing to be *watched*, with rhythm seen as a little triangle or square drawn by the conductor's hand winging out over the massed instruments of the orchestra. This prepotently visual sense (it is hinted by the diarist) makes difficulties for a soul such as his, which is best able to come to terms with existence as it was in the ancient world, when things stood still and the universal design was a static and comprehensible thing, when the earth stood firm and four-square on its corners. To trace the changing patterns of modernity, to grasp the rhythm of things that are constantly changing, endlessly shifting position, rushing through space - all this makes unbearable demands on a sensibility that is predominantly visual. For all Obstfelder's deep love and understanding of music, his imagination is nevertheless one which is most at home in a world where - whether directly visible, imaginatively visualized, or wholly visionary - vision is supreme.

Central to his sense of the age and its meaning was the image of the *swarm*. The swarm betokened for him a phenomenon which in respect of its constituent elements was bewilderingly random, dauntingly indeterminate, and in all practical senses unpredictable and yet which consolidated itself into a perfectly recognizable entity whose progression and direction through time and space was measurable and whose terminus could reasonably be plotted. The swarm thus represents a distinct shape, but a shape in endless internal flux, mysteriously held together by some inner power of containment, and as such peculiarly relevant to the newly emergent world-picture revealed by the discoveries of atomic and sub-atomic physics.

It is typical of Obstfelder that he should have oscillated between regarding *A Priest's Diary* as his masterpiece and seeing it as a melancholy failure. In its earlier stages of composition, he often felt that it was profounder than anything he had written hitherto - 'the weightiest, the richest thing I have written', he said in 1898. But shortly before his death, he had moments of complete despair of it: 'This book has come to be my misfortune. At one time I approached it with the greatest of expectations . . . . More and more a deep despondency has possessed me. I have misgivings about what I have done. It does not seem to me to correspond to what I had in mind, nor to what I still feel I might have been capable of . . . . And of late I have been and am seized by the deepest disgust for this book.'

That the work in its present form is both unfinished and unrevised to some extent conditions one's valuation of it as a work of literature. Where Rilke deliberately and for artistic reasons chose to leave *Malte Laurids Brigge* with its air of incompleteness, fate left Obstfelder no choice. Not only does *A Priests's Diary* lack its immediately concluding section, which Obstfelder estimated would take another three months to do; but even if it had been thus completed, it was probably intended to serve only as the first part of a larger work. It also lacks finish in a more metaphorical sense. Nevertheless it stands today as a work of extreme honesty, full of the immediacy of experience, and remarkable as much by the delicacy of its recognitions as by the resonance of its courage.

A PRIEST'S DIARY

What will stand at the end of this book? Will I have reached any conclusions? Will there be clarity in my mind?

I write to find peace. There is nobody I can talk to. My fellow priests? I know what they would answer. I have given myself the same answer. I have read the Bible over and over again. I have not read it in the right spirit, they would say.

No, I do not confess to my fellow priests. Is there not the great vault of heaven to confront? Staring, staring at me, and questioning. And crying out in the deep night.

I confess to myself.

I confess to that eye which is set deep within and which twice before in my life I have seen blazing.

*

This is my last attempt. I have prayed, I have brooded, I have read. My mind is going round in circles. I will write down my thoughts from day to day in an attempt to find out how they relate. And then? What then? What if I do not find the connection? What then?

*

Do the others not feel this terror within them when they stand before the altar?

When I raise the bread and the wine - his ... Christ's ... body and blood - when I bear these things to their lips, when the organ's response booms high under the vaulted roof, I see nothing, hear nothing. An infinite terror runs through me, a numbing cold. Would that all the heavenly bodies might suddenly come crashing down about me!

By all that is within me, by my entrails, my bowels, I offer the mystery to the trembling lips. I, the unclean.

I who know not how to resolve the smallest problem for these poor, poor people. Am I - I - expected to make them whole, to forgive them their sins?

How could I, how dared I do this, Sunday after Sunday, for four long years?

*

How glad I would be if I could turn to somebody, could tell all and hear their answer. I have been on my way to the bishop. I was driven back again. Something within me, above me, seemed to control me, to withhold permission, to hold me back. I must press on. I must reach finality.

When I meet any of my fellow priests, it is like being struck by lightning. *They* are the clear-eyed ones; they have a great optimistic faith. Am I not the world's greatest transgressor? Do I not violate what is most holy?

When I walk in the streets, I dare not look my fellow men in the eye. Yet I continue. Sunday after Sunday my ice-cold hand offers the bread and the wine to those who are more honourable than I. And nobody knows my shame. Nor my torment.

*

I lay awake last night. I saw the damned. I felt my hair turning grey and brittle.

I suffer along with each one of the damned. At this very moment yet another one goes to hell. One? No, many! Thousands! I feel the agonies, I suffer them, suffer them.

I see the tormented. I see them as they writhe. I see twisted faces peering out from corners. I see them staring at one another, watching the others' petrified despair. I feel time is endless. I take the place of the dead and tormented. I sense the infinite time of my own torment.

An icy chill lies about me, a darkness of blue, pallid faces, where clenched and bony hands stretch out.

Unclean thoughts flutter through the darkness, thoughts that have become flesh, that have eyes, that have claws - that stink, stink.

All about me are unclean thoughts, fetid thoughts, in every corner. They fly, they crowd in upon me, closer and closer. They settle on my eyes, settle on my tongue, creep down my gullet. Oh God, if you are good ... help me, help me!

*

Is this possible? Is this not hell, even before the judgement?

*

Who is this god? Let me see him! Let me see his face!

What is my transgression that I am chastised so harshly? Why am I punished more harshly than those who committed the sin?

I must see the face of this god! I must see what it is that he intends.

*

Yes, let me see you! You who hide yourself from us!

Question me! Tell me what I have done! And if I suffer for my ancestors' sake, for my brothers' sake, give me a sign!

Let me see the mighty dread! Let me observe!

Let me see that countenance of yours which turns men to stone. And then let me die and perish.

But let me see! Once only do I wish to see you, for one single moment! To look into your eyes and die. But first to have *known*, for one single moment.

Let me know my sin, let me see it clearly! And then let me depart hence. For surely I *am* already doomed. I, who have mocked! I, who have defied!

*

Is defiance my sin? As defiance was Satan's?

Is my defiance greater, more profound than that of all those others?

Have I derided that which is purest, the most sublime? That which must look with pain on all the world's loathsomeness.

Have I desired to see what none may see, none may approach, none dare witness except in the radiant garment of light, except in burning purity of soul, except in the searing power of the will?

Was it the infinite pity of the most great that preserved me from annihilation when I tried to approach him? Because he knew that, like the moth in the flame, I would be consumed if I tried to see him.

'Draw not nigh; put off thy shoes from off thy feet, for the place whereon thou standest is holy ground.'

'And Moses hid his face; for he was afraid to look upon God.'

*

Did Satan exist? Does he still? As a person? As the one from whom defiance derives, from whom universal strife is derived?

Perhaps all that *we* see is *his*? Are Satan's worlds? And God's we do not see.

And is this why they are full of sin, of sickness, of pain? And why there is darkness in nature, and poisoned serpent tongues, and fangs of savage beasts, and the devouring sea?

And perhaps there is also enmity among the worlds. Once before in time the peoples went in terror, waiting for the war of the worlds, for the bloody embrace of sun and earth, for the comets' conflagration.

*

No! A god - God - cannot desire my stupidity. A God cannot desire stupidity ... darkness.

God, who gave talents to all men, green shoots of the kingdom of the spirit. God, who set the seeds in the ground and caused the sun to warm them that they might grow and blaze in all colours when they unfolded. So that he might himself look upon them and rejoice at them and rejoice at his own greatness, saying: 'See, all is indeed well. See, all these things I did exceeding well.'

Omniscient is how I must think of Him. As the 'most intelligent' being, the wisest, the finest in thought, the noblest in judgement.

Do I invest him with *my* names? I invest him with the greatest I know. If I look for others, they are for me and for mankind lesser, poorer. To envisage him I must exert all my best powers, all my finest senses. No matter how wise I were, I would still be a simpleton by comparison with that infinitely sagacious and infinitely complex being wherein all things go, from whence all things come, and which yet comprehends them all.

Wiser than the wisest, infinitely wiser is how I imagine the All-Wise; purer than the purest, infinitely purer is how I imagine the Light. That he should not desire me to have the greatest understanding is something I cannot conceive; any more than that he should not desire the flower's growth. The higher I can raise my vision, the higher He becomes for me. The higher I see him, the more sublime and more ardent grows my yearning for what is purest and inmost. And the yearning itself is enhanced.

No, God cannot desire my ignorance, for only on the peak of wisdom's great mountain does the great yearning to see God, the

4

greatest of all things, begin. Can God be offended when one begins to glimpse his beauty, his prodigiousness - when one marvels and comes down from the mountain and proclaims across the world his greatness and the radiance of his person?

Perhaps on occasion a ray of light from the ultimate inmost sun reaches our earth and enters the camera obscura of the 'darkened understanding' - one single gleam. But this gleam begets the flower of eternal longing, the longing to know, to stand face to face and speak with the greatest, the fairest, the most radiant God.

Does God become greater by our being smaller?

Does God require us to act as simpletons so that he might seem so much greater?

*

Behind the muscles the tracery of bones, behind the green leaf the veins. Through the microscope, under X-rays, everywhere I see a plexus, a design. The lowest organisms are themselves the design, infusoria, plants.

With keener vision one would see - across the world, throughout the earth, within all nature, behind the veil of fleshy tissue - a splendid design of curving, sweeping lines, with the interstices filled with colour.

It would be like seeing an image of thought itself, the wave of thought, the law of thought.

And one would see a risen edifice, a temple over all space, would see living arches rear up and living lines entwine themselves strangely and ever more curiously.

The beginnings have the simplest lines. The stone has the basis of the law of thought, the square, the line's first note. But already square entwines with square, separates, elongates, craves new form. The flower, the star fish or the spider, even the crab ... to us their lines appear fantastic yet they are but the first initial convolutions.

Ever more delicate become the interlacements, more and more difficult to interpret the organisms' hieroglyphics, darker and darker the way to trace back to any origin.

Then the surrounding substance, the ambience - which itself fragments, variegates, and becomes ever richer and stranger.

And finally come heart and brain.

Imagine how it would be if, as a spirit, one could see the human body live, see the red blood with all its corpuscles coursing through the patterned mesh, see the lambent lines of the brain vibrant in the concert of thought's design and emotion's colour.

*

Sometimes I invoke this image:
Man walks upright on the earth, as though he of all beings would first raise himself from the dust and look up to other stars. Uppermost is his head, his brain.
Then I think of God sitting up there and looking down. Through the atmospheres, through the rings of light as seen from above, he sees the millions of brains, living, breathing. A glittering filigree, a sparkling, a trembling, a flickering of lights and colours and pictures. A strange vision!

*

I will exert all my powers that I might understand. There are times when I seem to see a ray of light streaming aslant into the dark chamber: I cannot trace it back to its sun. My senses are neither strong nor rich enough, my body inhibits me. But I have a faint inkling. And in any case I see things better in those moments than I normally do with my usual five senses.
At other times things remain in isolation. But when the stream of light invades, I become aware of certain threads which it was otherwise too obscure for me to see.
And instead of using my vision clearly and soberly to trace the direction and path of these threads, I become delirious at the beauty of the network of these rays of light - crossing and re-crossing, as the one speeds towards its neighbour, as it re-entwines itself in the old, as it never is and yet always is.
If only I could select one single thread, follow it, establish its connections.
How difficult it is to look! Difficult to look into the heart of light, into the source, from which the light is emitted to what is smallest and most distant.

*

It happened tonight on the way home. I was walking alone, just as all day I had been alone.

I am the last one out in the streets. The dark houses are different from what they are during the day; in the dark they seem to loom up like monsters.

My steps sound dully in the streets. The only sound.

Suddenly a cry. I feel compelled to go to it. I am drawn. What is it? I approach nearer, nearer. It persists. It is a moaning, a wailing, so aweful, so eerie there in the night.

What was it? Madness? Death?

Not at all. It was great joy. At that moment the world received a new son. A new soul took life among the community of souls.

*

That cry from the darkness sounds in my ears. In its terrible pain it sounded like some exquisite pleasure from the depths of the abyss.

What is there about it that makes me tremble?

*

Why am I so alone? Nobody clasps my hand. Nobody comes smiling towards me.

Is there a cast in my eye? Is there a sign somewhere on my brow that estranges me from those who are happy and at peace?

At times when I stand in a crowd of people, there is laughter behind me. And something pierces me through and through.

Logic tells me again and again: your loneliness is making you suspicious. They are laughing at their own small pleasures. And yet the laughter follows me right to my door.

It is as though tiny devils are following me, are between my feet.

*

That cry in the night!

A woman. My hand in a woman's hand.

A child that was *my* child ... out of me, out of my loins, out of my spirit ... my perpetuation ... my sacrificial offer to the earth!

Many women sit there below me when I preach. I have never thought about their being women. It is not that. That is not what Woman is.

7

I see them on the street. It is not that.

Love? Could I love any one woman now living on this earth?

I have seen women in old paintings. Did they ever really live? Or is it the artist's own vibrancy of soul that lies in that smile about their lips?

I never see any woman who smiles like that.

Is there any woman who is as I dream her, who has that great blue veil?

*

It is evening. Far away the church clock strikes its deep note. From other directions others answer. It is almost dark. A single white streak, almost at the earth's edge, where the sun went down.

And my soul walks over the earth, over its sweeping curve. My soul walks through the lands, looking, asking: 'Is there to be found any other soul like this? Is there anywhere a soul with which it can join, wherein it can vanish, and whereby this anguish of being, of thinking, of not understanding can be stilled?'

My soul finds no other that resembles it.

And my soul swoops into that distant white streak, and asks: 'Is there any other soul like this, into which it can disappear?'

Is there to be found, deep within, any person for whom my own soul will not be an *other*?

Or will that person there, deep within, address me as 'Thou'?

*

This is the terror and the fear : Will that one, deep within, say 'Thou'?

Will it, deep within, look on me as I look on my neighbour, look on me as something apart, something outside itself?

That is the terrifying thought.

*

Why did he leave us so wholly alone, he who created seed?

If we are intended to depart this earth as a mere component of it, as its dust and nothing more, to worship its loveliness then return to it, why were we given spirit - that spirit which ever desires to fly? Why were we

8

given the power to discriminate, to say 'beautiful', 'ugly'?

But if we are intended to transcend this earth - to be *more* than it, if we are beings who walk erect with our eyes turned to the stars because our way leads up there amongst them - then we are surely so alone, so very much alone. The firmament is a burden on every breast, the night a burden on every breast, and we cannot shake them off, cannot take them in our hands and bend them to our will.

*

True: 'the days of our years' are not many. But if it is all a game, a game with the planets, if death is only a little Christmassy door into a new room, to a new playtime, why should we then feel it to be so burdensome, so problematical, so weighted with responsibility, and so unending, this brief life here below?

*

There I was walking in the park. Under the old, high beeches it was pleasantly shady. People were relaxing. Were forgetting.

Then I saw coming towards me - guess who? The bishop. That was his snow-white hair.

I could not run away. Run away? Yes, I wanted to run away from his gentle eye! I was afraid of his benign countenance!

He came towards me, stretched out his hand. I dared not look at him. The whole time I felt his sun-bright eyes upon me.

He spoke. He said: 'My dear friend! You look despondent. Ah, yes! I know well enough that every man has his own problems, every man has his own gnawing thoughts. Ah! Such gnawing thoughts are the very devil!

'Are you not worrying just a little too much, my dear friend?' he then asked suddenly.

I seemed to melt inside, feeling that I should tell all, that I should speak out. Perhaps this old man with the white hair had experienced much of what now possessed me.

I stopped. I do not know how I brought it out. I said: 'It is very difficult.'

He also stopped. He placed his hand on my shoulder, and said: 'Explain yourself!'

I said: 'The way to God is very hard.' Where did I get the words?

Then he looked deep into my eyes, and a halo seemed to encompass the white locks that fell about his head, and he said: 'There is one name, my friend, which for me is like the touch of a gentle hand: Christ. Have you said that word to yourself, murmured it in the still night hour: Christ. Or have you ever whispered it to yourself when you saw the sun go down, sad and red: Jesus Christ.'

He seemed to fondle the word. A passage from the Gospels came vividly to my mind: 'Now there was leaning on Jesus' bosom one of his disciples, whom Jesus loved.'

But I could say no more. I understood nothing.

And he continued: 'For me religion was never without profound mystery. For me Christ is the mystery. And it is through Christ that I see God. Did He himself not say whilst He was on earth: "Through me ye shall see the glory of God; no man cometh unto the Father, but by me; I am the way to the truth and the life." That is the mystery: God transforms himself for us that he might be seen by our human eyes, comprehended by our human hearts. The God of love! That is Jehovah's new and glorious name! Yes, faith for me is like a delightful fairy-tale.'

He held out his hand. I watched him - this white-haired fairy-tale poet - depart with harmonious, peaceful steps.

*

Am I a son of darkness?

In the presence of these clear, transfigured countenances I feel like one with a curse upon him. It is precisely this peace, this harmony that I do not understand.

If I try to conjure up an image of him, Christ, white and radiant with the olive branch in his hands, I cannot bring it to realization. It grows dim, while a thousand confused thoughts chase round within me.

It is easy enough to grasp the doctrine: that by his death he brought about the great harmony in the world from out of its great disharmony. But I become confused: Why this dichotomy in time? An eternity in disharmony and then a new eternity in harmony? Is not time one, eternity one? I become confused. It seems to me there are so many problems attaching to this doctrine. But a doctrine which descends from the heavens to the peoples of all lands and times, must it not be simple? I become confused; I cannot see anything but disharmony, and I forget all else. I hear the drops of blood flowing under the earth and over the earth.

'He has redeemed us. He gave himself for us.' *He* was to accept punishment for the sins *we* had committed? No, this I do not understand. Would proud, free men not resist the idea of having their punishment indemnified by others? What kind of justice is this! What kind of God is this! Yes, in those moments when I try to picture him, try to comprehend him, I see only a mist before my eyes. I imagine there must be mystery upon mystery, darkness after darkness? Why is it necessary to have all these darknesses? Are there not burdens enough placed on our hearts and souls in this life here below? Is this great mystery of God not enough?

It seems to me that the New Testament ends in hallucination.

*

Out of this tormenting confusion some thoughts, new to me and strange, are beginning to take shape. They fill me with dread, for they are like shining lancets in all the old stuff one preaches. But as long as I am immersed in these thoughts, I find within me a great clear, cold peace of mind.

*

The people felt themselves to be alone on the earth. They saw sin and pain around them. They asked themselves, they asked one another: 'Why?' They did not know how to answer.

And there came the books of wisdom, the religions and the philosophies, which gave answer. Which said: 'Thus it was that it came to pass.' And each religion said of itself: 'I am the one that derives from the most ancient and the greatest God, I go back to the beginning. Believe me: thus it was that sin came into the world.'

And these books were handed down from generation to generation. But the people still felt themselves to be alone. The world was still full of enigmas. The miracle of birth brought ever new questions. Death cried out and bewailed the dread of uncertainty.

And the people felt withall a majesty in themselves. This was perhaps the hardest thing. This was the great tragedy.

They looked about them, saw the beasts, and said: 'We have all that they have, but we have much more!' They saw the beauty of the flower, and they said: 'We are even more fair!'

So why do we have this thing - this majesty - within us?

For we are not gods. We are halflings. We are unclean, and yet we love splendour. We are full of evil, yet we love justice.

Whence have we come?

And they asked: 'Will there not come among us one who is greater than all of us? One who has what we feel we can never attain yet which we tearfully hunger for? One who has clarity and is not possessed by fear?'

And they asked from generation to generation: 'Have you seen God? What was he like? What did he say?'

And the highest and most ardent spirits among men yearned for God. And Confucius came; Buddha came; Mahomet came.

And the prophets said: 'God was with us. Buddha was the son of God, Mahomet was the son of God.'

And they wrote it down, and it passed from generation to generation.

*

I wonder if there is perhaps a kind of philosopher's stone in our being so alone - I wonder if that is one of the mysteries of life here below?

Why should we expect to have all our problems given an immediate solution? For is our brief earthly life more than that little 'immediacy'?

Why is not death the mediator? Why is not death that which explains God to us, pointing the way to the truth and the life?

When it is a matter of searching for eternal laws, of the quest for God, what then is earthly life? Yes, what is the entire life of this terrestrial globe when the actual search is for one who created millions of planets? A being for whom the life of the planets is a matter of seconds.

If we have hope, is the search a long one?

It took generations before a single natural law could be established; it took centuries to realize the splendid vision of the planets dancing about the sun, of suns rushing through space. It took millenia to understand that sound and light and heat are oscillations, a rhythm of molecules. Yes, it took a thousand generations for man to understand a little about the human body. And even now what do we know of what goes on within our own brains?

Compared to the life of the stars, compared to the paths of the suns, how can this earthly life of humankind, told in finite numbers, be thought adequate for the search of him who filled the world with music?

Is it so long since Man raised himself from the dust and began to walk upon the earth, and began to look aloft? Often it seems to me as but yesterday, that morning of life on earth, when mammoths roamed the new-born planet. It seems to me like no more than this morning, those days when empires turned old and grey, and departed and died.

Surely we must seek not one but many lives. We must transform ourselves, seek with better light, perhaps approach - and ultimately find!

*

Should we give up the search? Since this earthly life seems to be too short?

We *must* seek. We cannot give up.

And as yearning we seek, and seeking we yearn, we are made new; we are raised up, higher and higher.

We *must* seek. It is a law of nature.

The more distant we are from that innermost centre of forces, from the omnipotent and the omnific, the more intense is our yearning. Because all is so cold. We still feel the pale radiance of some stars, still feel some of the forces from space or even something deep within ourselves. But oh! so enigmatic, so dark. If we were at some point in our quest to come closer, perhaps all our yearning would turn to radiant hope because of the nearness of the light; and in the end turn to fiery certainty.

Perhaps there may even be, within and beyond all our searches, an attractive force from that focal point from which are endlessly transmitted that infinity of rays to the myriad vital centres in the whole vast circuit of the universe.

*

If we have hope...

Indeed, why should we not have hope? Just as long as we see and live by that sun we cannot attain, and let our heads be bathed in light which comes from worlds we do not know and which it would take an eternity to reach.

As long as we continue to see that sun which is millions of miles from us, there will be blossom in the cotyledon, and steam in the coal and the driving of ships, and a photograph on the plate.

*

13

As long indeed as the god is himself ever changing, becoming ever greater, extending his sovereignty over more and more worlds, more and more creatures.

Or is the god of the age of the railway no greater than the one who merely possessed the world with its four corners?

He who turns the crank for millions of planets is mightier, more difficult to comprehend and to confront than the god who, in the Revelation of St John, caused his angels to cast down the stars of heaven upon the flat earth.

The god of the Egyptians was greater than the barbarians' idol; and that of the Jews greater than the Egyptians'; and greater still the god of Christ who sees into hearts and kidneys, and embraces all manner of peoples.

Greater, greater, greater.

*

And more distant.

It is as though he moves further and further away, rises higher and higher, as the world grows ever older and has learnt its course.

Already in the Bible it is thus.

In the Garden of Eden he walks like primeval man among the trees in the cool of the evening. He is the one spirit upon earth among all things which have begun to grow and have their being.

With the coming of man, he moves among them, is of them, grasps their hands, wrestles with Jacob as a man.

With the coming of Moses he grows; he strikes fear and conceals himself in the flame. The whole time he is issuing his commandments, Sinai trembles.

Then his appearances on earth become rarer; he prefers to appear in dreams, in visions, in ecstasies.

And finally, in the fullness of time, when the yearning to see God among men and to hear his voice has turned to a lament over the land, he does not come himself but sends his son.

Now that the earth is established, now that men themselves have begun to create, building towns and communities and making laws, it is as though he is himself far distant, deep within the cosmos, disposing over new worlds and making new laws in other realms.

His son comes in human form. The earth has grown so old that people are no longer able to see the person of God among them in material form. He has turned to spirit.

*

Did the earliest peoples, in the dark depths of time, still hold in their minds some recollection of a powerful spirit which had infused the earth with life and which had departed hence when they raised themselves from the dust and rubbed their eyes?

Was there any memory of a Jehovah who had visited the young planet and set life going upon it?

Was it the memory of a powerful spirit whose presence is still echoed for them in the rush of the wind through the tall trees in the cool of the evening, and to which the Indians gave the name of 'The Great Spirit'.

*

Now that very memory - if indeed it ever was - has receded. God has risen so high that we can no longer conceive of him. We were used to a God who had human properties. We could form a picture of him, and thus believe. But how can one have the flame of faith when one cannot picture any face?

God has become so enormous. The laws of nature have become so overwhelming in their structure. The god of the laws of nature cannot be a person, cannot be a Zeus or a Jehovah. To resolve the problem we make of him a spirit. But then so many new problems follow. How do we comprehend this spirit with all our being? And all this great material edifice - does he stand apart from it?

How can the ordinary person going about his tasks as he did thousands of years ago, tilling the land, wielding his plane, but having to live under countless new worlds and alongside new and powerful world forces - how can he picture to himself the power behind those powers, the miracle behind those miracles? He cannot see a person. He sees no hammer, no ninepins behind the thunder's fury. What is he to imagine? Man finds it so difficult - oh, so painfully difficult - to perceive anything with his mind and his soul other than what properly belongs to the world of that mind, to the realm of that soul.

Yes, He has drifted far far away. And in the deep of night when the hammers are at rest and before the machines awaken, in nights that circumfuse the earth's course as they did at the time of Abraham, silently as though nothing had happened, the sound of a sigh might be heard rounding the earth, a sigh from a single breast or from many: 'Where art thou? Art thou afar off? Art thou near me? Art thou like unto me'?

And many for whom this yearning grows too strong bend their heads and cast their reason in the dust and say: 'Cursed be thou, for thou hast stolen from me the image of God.'

And with that they cast into the dust what is perhaps the sublimest and purest memory of that spirit which departed in the morning of time.

*

Then the church rejoices. It is never so glad as when someone comes and says: 'It is not true that the earth revolves. It stands still. It is not true that the stars are worlds. They are just holes.'

Is God then glad?

Does his greatness increase if the earth stands still or if the stars are holes?

*

How strange! The greatest of mortal enemies the world has ever known is the church. That which was to raise the people up, and foster thought and the urge for truth within those same people. The church tortured Galileo, burnt Giordano! The church has killed the world's best men! The *church* has done this! Despite the fact that these men's ideas about God were the highest and purest that people have ever had.

Is there perhaps more of true religion in science which never believes it knows the whole truth than in theology with all its certainties?

Among the Chaldees astronomy was religion and the priests were scholars.

And now? Who are the true priests of this age?

Yes, there is religion in science. It extends space further and further, both outwardly and inwardly. It never ceases. It is forever searching. It is not content with man's innate senses: it invents the telescope to reach up higher and higher, and the microscope to penetrate deeper and deeper.

16

It permits us to observe the life of the world in all its power and glory, revealing ever higher aims within the universal purpose, leading us along the path where we can dimly discern something of the dimensions with which He worked, and in the depths giving us a sense of the mystery -a mystery of shining clarity with the brilliance of a million crystals.

*

I have thought. I have written. That has given me peace.

But when I raise my head, I am conscious of something behind those thoughts that torments me. It is fear? Is it want?

- Yet I am calmer. I feel the evening air. It invades my thoughts, cools my brow.

My window stands open. It is quiet in the streets.

At times I have a curiously strong feeling that I can hear a rushing sound from far off, from the age-old primeval forest, from the immeasurable sweep of the sea.

I have tall houses around me, streets, public buildings, theatres, stretching far and wide. But on some evenings it is as though a gust of air reaches me from some far distant place where it is wild and where there are things no human hand has planted.

And I get the feeling that this rushing sound is stealing in among the press of buildings, through the huddle of streets and such like - from the age-old primeval forest and the immeasurable sweep of the sea.

Imagine if the echo of this sound were to vanish from the soul of man. I do not know why but the thought of a time when Man has analysed and re-cast all things makes me shudder with fear.

A time when the face of the earth is covered with buildings and schools and kitchen vegetables, and when the waves of the sea are by some trick reduced to silence.

I think my heart could not beat if I did not know that somewhere - be it never so distant - my soul might encounter wild forest that no human hand had planted.

*

It has begun already. It began long ago. Iron snakes its way through the soft moss, crushing the poor little wintergreen in its path. Iron horses drive the red deer from their pastures. The last children of the forest are driven away, the red man poisoned, the black man enslaved.

Soon the buildings will creep across the pampas, telegraph poles be rammed down among dead roots, a network of copper wires strung out where branches once wove their summer-glad tracery.

Then that rushing sound will vanish! That sound which infiltrates Man's most ancient and immortal soul and induces memories. It takes us to the forests of the Mohicans, to the islands of the Pacific. Like a whisper of the gods it passes over the earth on Midsummer Eve. Yes, on midsummer nights it again sweeps proudly over the earth. But at break of day it is banished, driven out to sea, there to find refuge in the strangely contorted shells of the Pacific.

If there are arteries running through the earth, if living streams flow within its belly, surely then I think it would die, whisper a last sad lament and expire. Die - like a living body overwhelmed and consumed by bacteria.

*

A feeling of dread grips me that I may not be able to embrace it and possess it before it dies.

There are still forests out there, still tall oaks with their ample crowns, still palms along the sun-white shore, still the young rivers leaping over the stones, wild and untamed.

And I feel I must go there. I must have the whole sun, the earth's sun. I must have the whole sea, must kiss the flower's fragrance, must drink the sap of the leaf.

Is Nature inside our minds? Seeing that I who have sat year after year with my books feel these vibrations? Is there something in my mind which drank its first mother's milk out there? Which has Nature as its primordial mother?

Why do we never speak any more of the God of Nature? Why is he withheld from us?

Was ever a more splendid god depicted anywhere than the one who speaks to Job from out of the whirlwind?

'Hast thou commanded the morning since thy days; and caused the dayspring to know his place?

Canst thou bind the sweet influences of the seven stars, or loose the bands of Orion?'

Or where in his proud might he calls out to Job concerning the leviathan he himself had made - he, the only one without fear:

'By his neezings a light doth shine, and his eyes are like the eyelids of the morning.

Out of his mouth go burning lamps, and sparks of fire leap out.

Out of his nostrils goeth smoke, as out of a seething pot or cauldron.

His breath kindleth coals, and a flame goeth out of his mouth.

In his neck remaineth strength, and sorrow is turned into joy before him.'

And yet. Let the earth die.

Let it be born, grow, become old and die.

Let the countries die!

Often I read of how men are afraid their countries might die and communities perish.

Is it not their lot to live, flourish and die? As it is with people?

Shall they not all live and die, France, Russia, England, like those which earlier died, one after the other, Egypt, Greece, Spain?

Why do we pour scorn on dying countries? Countries which are dying often bring forth blossoms which are the finest they ever produce. From their graves the new peoples gather them in.

He who created the swamps is not tight-fisted.

Let them die. There is the wherewithal for new primeval forest.

Thousands of new stars can be showered down for every one that vanishes. There is splendour. A structure that falls in ruins sinks only to make room for a more glorious one. There is pride.

Human beings are poor. They suffer under their poverty. Wealth is something unknown. They are fearful of losing.

*

But I must up and away and see it before it dies! I must climb a high mountain and look out over Mother Earth!

I must see the forests that are ordained for death. I must hear the thunder rolling from peak to peak, see Jupiter's lightning flash in the cloud, kiss the wet earth where no foot ever trod.

*

That railway station!

It makes me sick at heart. It plunges me into a turmoil of thoughts. And I know not what to do.

The darkness under the curving roof, the lights in the darkness, the locomotives screeching back and forth - to me it is like some mystery.

The mystery of modern life.

Man has become a new creation. His heart has a different beat. It beats to a new rhythm.

Formerly people remained still. They grew like plants and flowers. Now they are torn from their soil. They are near to flying. But they are not yet birds. That is why it is like the fluttering of birds which are sick and near to death.

A journey is no longer what it was. Formerly it was a way of life. Now it is merely a little movement, a turning, an oscillation.

When I stand and look into the strange area within, where blinding lights suddenly emerge from the darkness, I feel in the end as though I am looking into all the new music of life. People move back and forth, in and out and past each other, never at rest, like molecules in an incandescent gas.

Century of music - century of the railway.

On the move, on the move. They cannot think one thought through to the end, cannot sustain one feeling through to the end. The man leaves his wife's bed, and the children their mother's breast.

Finally I see all mankind in one single swirling vortex - and I become sick at heart. Is there then no rest, no peace, no repose any longer on earth? Is there no *home* any more in the world?

*

Then suddenly I can be so happy knowing one place that does stand still: chairs that stand where they stood last year, tables where my old books lie summer and winter, books I have lived with for years. The Bible, that strange and dangerous Bible! Pascal, whom I cannot understand and who must belong to a different world from mine, having a different soul and a different body! Kant! Darwin!

I enter. I shut the door. And it seems to me so peaceful, so very beautiful. A little patch of sky comes in at this window, sometimes casting a shadowy black cross on the table. A patch of sky to remind me of the oceans. How often have I not sat there by the hour just watching the light from the sun that was too high to come down into the narrow street, or watched Venus, Mars, Charles's Wain.

Here I am alone. Nobody can disturb me. There is peace here. Peace for a moment, at all events. For half an hour. Peace, peace.

And my eye falls on my camellia. One never grows tired of looking at flowers, at corollas that one has seen burgeon and unfold, of kissing stamens that belong to one. My camellia is singularly rich in blossom. It does not shed its blooms as camellias generally do.

Yes, this is *my* world: these books, this window, this camellia. It is *mine*. Here *I* am master. There is nothing here but *me*. There is nothing here to come cutting its way into my soul, to disturb.

Is that possible?

God is omnipresent! He follows me everywhere. He is standing in here looking at me. His eye follows me. I cannot run away.

Is that possible?

Not even here am I alone. It is *not* my world. I am *not* the one who is master here.

He follows me everywhere with his implacable eye. Were I to flee even to the edge of the world, to the mountain's cave, he would follow me, transfixing me with his glance.

He is here, in this room, beneath the table, sitting on this sheet of paper. He follows everything I do, sees everything I think. I do not see what *He* does; I do not know what He thinks. He knows me. I do not know him.

Why am I to be humiliated thus? What have I done that my every nerve quivers with a sense of degradation and humiliation? Why does this all-mighty being want to trample on me?

*

And yet. Let him, if he so wills it!

In which case he must be wretchedly unhappy. Wretchedly unhappy if he is to be in every hapless person's chamber, sharing his thoughts, feeling his distress.

Has God no power *not* to be here? Is he *compelled* to be omnipresent?

I can avoid watching what I do not wish to see. I can avoid going where I do not wish to be.

*

He is here, omnipresent, in my chamber.

That is terrifying.

Why does he not speak, not call out to me?

Or does he call? Does he call day and night, in the evening when I retire, and in the morning when I rise?

Does he call within my own Self? Is he within my own Self? For there is always something within, watching. And I recall two moments in my life when it seemed as if an eye was seated deep within, an eye older than my own Self, older than my mother, watching me, watching.

Might he be within me? Might there be a part of God within there? A part only, for there is a dread, an embarrassment, a fear of seeing Him whole.

Why am I tormented by the thought that I am not alone, not master here?

And why am I tormented by the thought that God is in me as a part of me?

Was I not in fear and dread that this presence deep within me might address me as 'Thou', and regard me as an intimate?

*

Might there not be some comfort in the thought that he is here, and that I always had a companion? Who was of my soul, of my being?

Surely he would not see only evil in what I did.

He would see me caress the camellia. That surely cannot be sinful.

In truth it is his camellia. When I bow my head to the camellia, do I then not bow it to him? Do I not kiss the nails on his feet? Did roses not bloom where he left his footprints in the earth that first summer night?

*

We torment ourselves, brothers and sisters! Day and night we see only what is evil. We rend ourselves, lacerate the glorious work which God's spirit created and which his hand assembled. We rend it till it bleeds, dismember it, observe it with lens and with microscope, asking: 'Is there sin there? Is there impurity? Is this not vice? Is that not pride?'

Perhaps God smiles occasionally, thinking we take things too far.

How else could he endure it? Sometime perhaps, when a woman stands before him trembling in all her limbs for the dark sinfulness of her life, he will say: 'Woman, do you recall that evening - Venus stood in the sign of Cancer - when I saw you kiss that rose. You were alone. Nobody else saw you. Woman, one of my angels was in that rose.'

Perhaps it is God alone who can feel and see what is good.

*

It is strange. Man can endure the sight of his wretchedness. Is ready to contemplate it. He feels no reluctance about looking at his stinking burden.

He is reluctant to see the good in himself. At the silent hour when Man stands in judgement upon himself and something seems to emerge which may have been good and deserving of credit, he does not wish to look at it. He recoils, embarrassed. He turns his eyes elsewhere.

Is God the only one who may watch some noble act of mine without my being hurt by the knowledge that it was seen?

We are loth to see what is pure in ourselves. We fear to see God's countenance. Is that the same thing?

Is the light from the smallest molecule of goodness so strong that the human eye cannot bear the brilliance?

Is it the remnant of some image of God we are loth to see?

Or see again?

*

There is something inside of me that resists the notion that I am not alone.

I *will* be alone here in my room. I cannot *abide* the idea that someone is looking at me unbidden.

I was fearful I might not meet a soul-mate. I tremble now at the thought that I might not confront, deep inside me, a being who is outside me, and who will take my hand and address me as 'Thou'.

My mind reels!

Why must I think these thoughts? Why am I lashed by the Furies of thought. Why am I the one who has to think all these thoughts?

What do you want of me? Why do you pursue me? Why do I feel you suddenly on my couch at night in my arms? What do you want with me? What have I done? Why do you hunt me? Was it I who plundered the flame? Was it I who stole the thought in the apple?

But I will not be cowed. I will not be forced to bend the knee.

Am I expected to drag myself along in the dust like some miserable worm?

*

Forgive me. If you are there, forgive me for what I wrote yesterday.

Amen.

*

Is it then the case that all human beings are parts of one body? Is there some broken navel-string joining me to all other mortal beings, painfully twitching and giving me no rest.

Why can I not be alone? If I try to raise myself up towards the light, something draws me back to my fellow men. I sit here quietly, yet to my heart it is as though I were part of mankind's dance of death. As they all go whirling away like molecules in an incandescent gas, I feel my own spirit suddenly taking off and I have no peace of mind.

It is as if the telegraph and telephone wires were all strung through my head. That rushing sound above the roof-tops courses through my brain. All the thoughts of the multitude, their sighs, their lamentations penetrate my heart. I writhe in my bed. I want to hide myself away from it all, and cannot.

*

But this evening I remembered something curious.

This morning I went out early. I could not sleep. I saw people I have never seen the likes of before. I saw thousands of young men and women. Many had tormented faces. Others had not slept but had used the night for pleasures for which the day gives them no time. Their hair was dishevelled, their eyes were heavy. I watched them as they plunged into factories, disappearing between driving belts and wheels.

And more and more woke and hurried off to work: those who forge and carpenter and sew, those who make food and clothing and furniture, those who distribute to millions of mouths and hands.

Only *I* had no part in it. There they were: people stretching out their hands, raising roofs to the sky, throwing arches across the waters, combining and helping each other to build the world greater, richer and ever stranger, from the vision of their brains and the urgency of their will. And *I*...I do nothing. I stand outside; I do not belong with them. Their hearts would not understand me.

I did not dare to let my soul approach them there. I did not know anybody there. *My* god is not the others' god. *My* god - who is *my* god? Did I not defy? Did I not mock?

- I walked through the parks. I felt as though my foot had no right to tread the paving stones which the compassion of the community had set down, or that I might breathe the fragrance of the trees it had planted.

And I was ashamed to look these people in the eye, each hastening to his objective, each to his beneficent labours, eager, earnest, staunch or glad and strong, confident.

Then a woman, a mother, happened to come walking along. She had a little child in her arms.

And see! It stretched out its arms towards me! It smiled at me!

And I smiled back!

And it turned its head and looked at me the whole time with deep, clear eyes; and it smiled at me and stretched out its two tiny, infant hands towards me. As though it knew me.

It was after all only a little child. Yet a tremor ran through my whole body. I felt that my blood was red and warm, that it leapt in my veins and with every second was born anew from the secret springs and wells of my body.

The clear eyes of that child have been with me the entire day. I believe I shall sleep tonight. That the whining of the steel wires up there must cease.

*

Christ!

He held out his hands over the heads of the multitude. He felt the urge to extend them over all mankind. He said they were one body. He taught us the words: brothers and sisters.

Were they God's new words?

Was he God?

*

One evening last summer I was walking past a garden. I saw a whole family sitting there round a spread table. On it was a white cloth. Steam rose from the tureen. The lady was preparing salad. The children looked so happy. They laughed and chattered.

I crept near and watched. It was a lovely sight.

Ah, but there was something in their voices that hurt!

Something warm and fresh and at the same time soft. But in *my* heart it hurt.

Imagine being in there! Among them! Among those who build society - strong, staunch, happy people! Imagine being in there!

*

Christ!

I see him in my mind's eye. He holds out his arms over millions of bowed heads.

I see him. He smells an olive leaf.

I see him. He sits between his two friends in Emmaus' inn.

*

Christ, the bishop, my brother clergymen, the good people, they all stand there with radiant faces.

And I tremble and flee. Flee in anguish!

*

'Come unto me all ye that are weary and heavy laden.'

Was he God?

*

'Come unto me all ye that are weary and full of pain.'

They are some of the most beautiful words in the world.

But I have no wish to be weary! I wish to raise my head and seek, even though it were in the weariness of death.

'It is good to be weary and exhausted by the vain search for the highest good so as to be able to stretch out one's arms to the Saviour,' says Pascal.

That I do not understand. To me there seems to be something of spiritual bankruptcy about it. Is Christ to be a God for the sick and enervated?

There is something weak, something sickly and ingratiating in Christianity which repels me and which I feel cannot be the truth. The gentle face of Jesus in the oleographs nauseates me. The faces of the lay preachers enrage me. These artificially gentle and soft voices of the converted hold something I instinctively feel to be spurious.

*

To the Christian, Christ is God. In private it is the Son incarnate one is with. He knows him, knows what he is like, knows his face is human. It looks down upon him with gentle reproach, with kindly sympathy. The Christian always knows what that look will be: reproachful, sympathetic, or comforting.

I do not understand that. And since I do not understand it, it does not fire me.

Life is robbed of its great dread, its tremendous majesty, when the name I encounter in my privacy is not Jehovah's. And my humanity can invoke and be at one with only one of them. I cannot be at one with God, Christ and the Holy Ghost all at the same time. That is too many great powers for one poor mortal creature. It makes my mind reel and lose control. Why does one need so many?

*

I feel that Christianity has removed God from the earth. Christ is the mediator. He is to be God for us, because him we can comprehend.

So do we want one we can comprehend when we cast ourselves down in the dust before the most high? To a child its father is a Jehovah, not a Christ. On the ocean of eternity I am as a child. There is something in me that resists the idea of entrusting myself in surrender to a human being, to somebody like myself.

Does not the human soul - in its yearning, its sobbing entreaty -ask for the most ancient of gods, the very fountain head?

Christianity came to ease the burden. Should it be eased? Life is after all not easy. Its purpose is not easy. Human nature is not easy.

Perhaps Christianity is idolatry like all the others? The last and most dangerous of them? Perhaps Christ was the last God that Man made in his own image.

*

Did God also send Christ to other planets?

Was he also born there into the chosen generation of a chosen people?

Would Christianity have arisen in an age when people believed in the existence of other worlds, with life inspired by Jehovah's breath?

*

Mostly it is two things that urge one to Christianity: weariness or fear.

It often seems to me therefore to lack pride.

Christ's help is sought against fear: fear of punishment, of death, or of loneliness.

Can a Jehovah love those who come creeping, pale with fear or dispirited with weariness?

*

Fear is the state of human degradation.

Sin is the greatest thing on earth. Greater, mightier is the sin Man commits than the good he is capable of doing.

Sin makes men tremble and bend the knee. Napoleon's campaign in Russia was one of mankind's greatest sins. No human action has caused more pain. Yet people have bent the knee before Napoleon in admiration and terror, as before no other person.

I often long to meet a being who is without fear. His countenance must shine as with a thousand suns.

Fear is darkness.

*

Why do I exist? What is it all for? Why do I encompass worlds when my body is a worm?

One small stab, one little jerk at the thread of life and all would be over.

I am nothing. The slightest thing can cause me trouble and pain. A stomach twinge causes me more pain than a anguished thought.

There are millions of lives like mine. Millions of heads that think. So what am I doing?

What is all this for? Why do I hold it so urgent to have all things decided, to have my soul rightly aligned with the whole cosmos?

*

Yes, what am I? A farm hand, a messenger boy is worth more than me. There is slime in my mouth, a yellow cast to my eye. My skin is green.

Since I cannot die yet, suppose I were to go to sea? Took a job as a sailor? Then I could hold up my head, then I would have a decent job, then colour would come to my cheeks. Yes, and then my thoughts could rest. I could stand on watch at night with the eternal silence around me, with that vast and splendid space all around, feeling strong and well. I would have no need to think, no need to feel ashamed in front of anyone.

But no! I cannot, I must not.

How happily I would! How happily would I not run away! From this room, from this window, from these books, from these nights! Oh, these nights!

*

Should I? This very day, even now as I think about it? Immediately. For why should I be tormented so pointlessly? Someone has already suffered for the sins of mankind.

I can do no more. I cannot think straight. I am no use to anybody, not even to myself. Who has need of me? People? God has not.

Down past the wharfs. The riggings. Out into the unknown. Not another thought for months. Only the sea breeze, the salt sea air, in both nostrils, on the palate, and spume in the eyes.

Am I not right? To give it up. What am I doing here on earth if not to live an earthly life?

*

I am frozen. I am not yet dressed. It is morning. Six o'clock. I am sitting in my shirt. Dressing oneself is a slow business. I am so listless. I can only write. A few lines now and then. Why do I write this so meticulously? Who is going to read it?

Actually it is splendid to write like this. It is a great discovery. One occasionally jots down a few lines. Then one is free. Then the brain rests again. But then from far away come the thoughts, one by one, gently stealing, whispering. They come in droves, in shoals, in great processions. Again and again they come thronging. Then one must seize them on the instant, every one, everything, not one of them must escape the net. Not one - for it might be the missing link in the chain.

Get it written down. And go on. In this way it cannot come back again.

- Oh! I no longer know what I am writing. The pen moves, the hand moves, simply to write, simply so that my own self can find a moment's rest. This weariness, this weariness - this is the thing I fear most.

*

One has small pleasures. They become large.

The coffee is simmering. Ah, that smell, how good it is! Did I write that? Why did I have to write that? It is of no real concern. It has nothing to do with what I am seeking. That's not what it is all about. Write, pen! Write!

All right: I am alone. I dismissed my housekeeper. I see to everything myself. I wanted to be alone so that thoughts could come. That I could be so completely quiet that not one could escape. Thoughts. And echoes deep in my breast.

It fills the whole room. How strange! Coffee from Arabia, tea from China, oranges from Italy, fish from the sea, meat from the land - the whole world in our bellies!

*

I cannot forget it.

I woke. I felt a pain stabbing in my breast. And a weight beyond measure. I was afraid. Afraid of that terrible thing that often comes in the night and tears at me. Lust.

I felt forgotten, alone on the earth; everybody had left, and the other planets had rolled away.

I raised myself up. I did not want to feel. No, I did not want to think. I wanted to look out, to find light outside. I stared about me. It was dark in the room.

Then something happened. I saw a face, blue-pale, staring in the dark. I saw two eyes. I saw its bristling hair. Only moments later did I realize: it was my own face. In the mirror. Opposite my bed.

I had not seen it for several weeks. I dared not look at my face in the mirror.

Never in my life shall I forget it. The sight of my face.

I got up and dressed. I sat in the armchair. Time slipped by; hours passed. I was not aware of time. That was good.

Then came the morning light.

*

What is sin? And what is not sin?

When this urge in my body grows so powerful, when it goes surging through my soul and says: 'I will! I will!'

What is sin? Is it not that urge which is in the soil, in the trees, in the flowers, in all things that live and grow and put forth colour -- is it not that urge which lives?

Maybe it is sinful when I suppress it within me?

But where to go? When I look about me, I do not see anything on the face of the earth that meets my desire. I do not see the eye that would set my blood coursing, my soul crying: Hallelujah!

*

Why does it keep company with the dark? Why does it run down my spine like dread? Why does it hide itself in black night? Why does it so often have sin as its consequence?

I do not understand.

*

I have been along by the quayside. A wave of ecstasy surged through me. Free, foot-loose, out in that salt air that my lungs hunger for.

Away from it all. Into new worlds.

The very thought brought deliverance as I walked along there, as my eye strayed over that beautiful web of rigging, cordage, ropes, ladders, sails.

Just imagine standing up there, like a bird almost, at the height of the storm! And with no fear of death. Others might have it perhaps, but not I. Proud in the storm! At home there!

But as I walked up and down there, something strange happened.

Suddenly my head raised itself and my lips spoke out loud: 'I will not!'

And it was as if somebody had seized me by the scruff of the neck and said: 'If you run away, you are a coward!'

*

But later that terrible weariness returned. As if my mind was dying. I just had to sit down. I sat there for hours. I looked at a flower bed. Just to have something beautiful to look at. A lovely colour can be such a good thing when the mind is sick.

*

Now it is night. One o'clock. I have been wandering up and down, up and down. I dared not go home where I was this morning, and the previous night. In the end I was driven - into battle - once more.

I am still restless. I can hear my heart beating loudly. Often when it is very quiet, I get the disturbing feeling that this heart is some other being. An unknown being. It has a mind separate from you; it is an independent being, a personality different from the one that thinks and sees.

Why do you beat like this, heart? You beat - and I don't know what it is you want.

Thinking of this world, of this great immeasurable world, I wonder if there is anywhere where thoughts can find rest and this painful hammer-blow beating can be stilled. A memory? Do I not have some good bright memory to which my mind might drift and find rest?

- I come in through the door of my silent room, opening it cautiously. It was then that my heart began pounding. I halted in the darkness. *Is* there somebody there? Did I hear steps?

I move forward. Suddenly a tremor runs through me from head to toe. A foot. A light shuffling footfall. Somebody is there.

The next moment I realize it is only the open window rattling.

I light the lamp. Again a sudden faint noise. From the bedroom. What is the matter with me? My heart is pounding within me.

I light the table-lamp. Light the hanging lamp in the other room. I light the lamp in the bedroom.

Lights, lamps, everywhere! Light! light!

I walk up and down. My breast was heaving - it still does - as though some great passion had gone surging through it, as if somebody had caused me great pain or faced me with a difficult choice. I pace up and down, until at last a deep wondrous peace comes over me. More than that: a festive joy, a swelling rapture. And again my heart pounds, but differently.

And all at once amidst all the lights I have lit there appears a fiery image which my mind has evoked.

Is the mind - the thing which sees through what is impenetrable, which feels what is distant, which reaches out to what once was but is now believed dead - is it itself a flame?

- It is the Himalayas that rise up before me. The Himalayas in the burning sun. But it is not a grilling, flickering flame up there. There the sun is pure light. The dazzling brilliance of all that white expanse is noble and serene.

I stand atop the peak of Everest itself. No human life for miles. No towns, no smoke, no traffic noise, no bad air.

But in this immense solitude I am not lonely. Nor do I feel small. I stand up there and rejoice, waving my hand to the shimmering blue...reaching into that shimmering blue.

And I am seized by a powerful feeling: My mind is in that sun. My mind *is* the sun.

My mind undulates to the same splendid rhythm as the sunlight. See how, out there in the sparkling light, it dances across the snow crystals, dividing and again dividing, into two, four, sixteen...into millions of new ones, leaping up and down in myriad ranks.

Yes! it too, like the sunbeams, can refract into colours - not just seven but seven times seven, ever new, endlessly different.

It seems my heart will burst with joy: at the mind's majesty, its omnipresence, its creative power. Wave after wave after wave...

What does it want? What does my heart desire?

Someone to talk with? Some mind in which to ignite a flame from the flame given to mine?

*

We torture ourselves. We flay what was in its time 'created in God's image'. We rend it till it bleeds. We sorrow, we suffer. Dark thoughts weigh down our heads towards the earth. We no longer see the sun, the blue of the sky.

Perhaps that is a sin? Perhaps the greatest? Should we not be exulting and rejoicing? God lives, the planets follow their course, the flowers send forth fragrance, colour begets colour, the rainbow gleams. Should we not sing?

Perhaps he who made it all, who created the eye and ear of mankind, is a little offended, who knows? At the fact that we have time for lament as the roses bloom. That we do not stand looking with marvelling gaze, our eyes filled with tears of ecstasy.

We say how nice the weather is today. We say what lovely sunshine, and oh! just look at the full moon. But our hearts are not moved. We do not cast ourselves down to give thanks, thanks, thanks.

*

Sometimes we feel a tremor within us; only faint perhaps, but a distinct tremor. In sympathy with something we are ignorant of, something deep within, at the very heart of light, of the flame. Sometimes we feel vibrations, a kind of dancing, a throbbing response to something far distant, something unknown, something deep within, dancing in the universal dance, joining in the universal hymn.

We are part of it, we live, only faintly perhaps, pale, like the foetus. But we do live, we do belong.

And we feel our minds within us, we feel our minds about us, an ambience. We feel it stretching, swelling, putting out wings. We see our thoughts shining, sparkling, flashing. And our hearts! Hearts that play and laugh and weep! Hearts which today were withering as though they wished to die, yet which tomorrow will be so full, so flushed, so ardent and warm.

Yet we do not rejoice! Why do we not walk over the earth in broad array, and raise green branches to the blue sky, and open wide our throats and lift our heads to the larks and join in their chorus?

Yes, we are part of it all! We are part of universal life! We are not in death! Yet we do not rejoice!

*

Choking pain, torturing thoughts, are they things of evil? Things of the dark? Is it joy and light that God craves? Radiant faces, laughing eyes? Does he wish to see heads held high, people who have defied their agony, conquered the embrace of darkness, and who raise their eyes to the sun and smile through their tears? Men and women who never drag their feet, but whose footsteps trip lightly over the earth in rhythm with the sunbeam and the budding flower, with the joyful song of the birds and the tempestuous wave?

What is his wish? To see the defiant battle against sickness and pain? The final victory in sunlight and joy? To see the growth of that faint inner sensitivity which responds, unfolds, luxuriates, matures and finally sustains itself without pause? Does he yearn to see it develop into the music of life, to that which remained after what the Bible says was created in his image, and to see it embraced, succoured, and grow in majesty?

*

We inherited the earth. The earth with the Mediterranean and the Atlantic and the great Pacific ocean in the east. It envelopes itself in light. With every second, with every breath we take, there is a plenitude, an abundance of new birth and new life around us. Round the whole wide world there is a sphere whose cells are life-cells, vibrating, trembling, throbbing with life, life, life.

The people should kindle beacons from peak to peak over the whole of this earth. Away over the corn and the reddening fruit a cry should roll from hearts that are full: 'This is ours! We live, we breathe, we exist!' The present clings to the present. There is a growing and a decaying, a giving birth and a dying. There *is* not death. Not silence, not emptiness. There is radiance from a million lights that are living worlds. Air, water, they teem with cells. Trembling, teeming, burning, living, living, living.

Human beings should kindle a flame in all their blood springs, and should laugh to the light: 'We love, love.'

*

Yes, sometimes I feel a stirring within me, lowly creature though I am. In my mind and in my body I sense the hint of the vibrancy and the fire of the suns. How terrible if I should die for all time, and vanish without that trembling life having had a chance to grow, without my having joined in the great dance.

Could this thing happen here? Here on earth?

Was that what God wanted? That we should all grasp hands, all of us: first the few for whom the light had shone, then more and more drawn in by those few, then all - all hand in hand combatting the dark, bearing flaming swords against distress and suffering, and then to gather together from North Pole and South to cry out to heaven: 'We regained the earth. It sails on with no contrary winds. Ahead under full sail!'

*

I yearn for the world of my childhood. The sun that shone over me then, the evening star that rose above the grove, the grass I lay in. What I saw, what I heard, what I breathed in, these things I want to see, to hear, to breathe in anew. It is as though something had gone out of me, as though I had been living in a dream, as though I would find myself again when those things which were then around me and within me returned again. Then there would be peace, great peace.

*

I heard music. The Parzival overture. It was like the song of the very heavens themselves. A mighty chorus of great horns and powerful strings; yet it was not an assault on the ear, for it made a surging harmony. No dissonances; nothing that changed. It was like an eternal one-and-the-same, and yet it was not dead.

I was never able to understand how great happiness could be peace.

But in this music there is both peace and yet also surging change and surging loveliness. Here a man has looked out beyond the human range of vision. He has known a divine urge. There is sun in this sea of notes, sunlight and suns, rays of a thousand colours, vibrant strings that gambol and play about the great suns, the mighty trumpets.

*

Why should the heaven of salvation not be a place? Why should it not be as it is for children's minds - a heaven high up there among the Christmas stars, a heaven far off beyond the Milky Way? Would we be able to dream of an Olympus if not upon a mountain, or a Paradise if not in a garden?

Yet it *has* become a fairy tale world for the human mind, has it not - this heaven far beyond the Milky Way? There, at the distant centre of all space, it sees those eternal forces driving the wheels of the universe. Could it be perhaps that *there*, where the eternal forces reside, modern man might feel on his own nerves a new and radiant salvation? Surely this heaven has become large enough, grown enough surely in height and depth. Room enough there surely for the most defiant of souls - the kind of soul that tolerates no limitations, no fetters!

Often I have a feeling that my feet are starting to climb, that I am able to raise myself up from the earth, that the cells of my body are distending and filling with an ethereal delight. I feel I could surely spread wings and fly. I cannot. But to me it feels like the first drum-beat that heralds new world forms, heralds a paean of the body and of the bloodstream beyond the frontiers of the human mind.

Why should these drum-beats of the morning sound within us mortals if that day is never to come? If there is to be no onward movement? Felt in every pore? If the *great* rejoicing is never to be? The one which is without tears? If the great *quaking* is never to be? The one which never grows weary or exhausted?

People often say: great joy can never last. For *that* is part of the nature of great joy. And is that not the very night of earth: that joy cannot exist without *diminuendo*, cannot be sustained, cannot remain at the same pitch?

Why have the white nations cast away the dreams that all the peoples of the world once had in all the world's corners? Perhaps there was some truth in those dreams of a life without night, of a life where the sun of joy shone day after day and living entities remained vibrant at the highest pitch of pleasure, tireless, like an orchestra holding a sustained harmony within which all instruments are joined.

We see all things about us changing. We see indeed nothing but change.

Why are we no longer able to dream of new and radiant beings or a new and shining heaven?

*

I walk past leafy gardens; and I feel as though only one fragrance can bring me peace, one faint delicate fragrance that stole over me in the morning of my life, a faint delicate fragrance.

I feel that I failed to immerse myself in it properly then, failed to breathe deeply of it. Now it is lost. Now perhaps it can never be found. I could have drunk it in through every pore, and I failed.

I wonder if *that* is happiness: to feed one's eyes over a long long time, maybe forever, with the same colours. To breathe in the same ether. Everlasting peace!

Is this our judgement: the unrest of our earthly life, the spirit's unrest, humanity's harassment? Is it this which is our judgement?

*

Once there was peace. At that time the earth stood still.

Now it moves, speeding on through space as though whipped. And we move with it. All our ideas - indeed more, all our powers, all the feelings within us. At one time life was peaceful, composed of settled forms with no anomalies to cause confusion. There was steady growth: not this intertwining, this turmoil of aggregate states, this endless shifting. Everything moved at a steady pace, day and night, summer and winter, the budding of the leaf, the withering of the leaf. And there was no thought that this steady pace would ever change. No thought of the restless circulation of the sap within the plant, of millions of cells in rapid combustion, of the inflow and the outflow of acids.

There were four elements, not many. Nor any one with the ability to transform itself into thousands. There were four elements as there were four seasons and four corners of the earth. It was two, and four, and two times four. It was not the round decimal's wider and wider circles. It was the square; it was not the circle, the cornerless, the endless.

And it was from these ambient things that Man was also compounded, from the elements as they saw them: earth and air and fire and water. Had anybody seen the nervous system? Nerves which for us are always vibrating, whose repose is but an interval in the pursuit of life. Nerves which even our children know and call telegraph wires - telegraph wires along which telegrams flow incessantly back and forth.

*

There is a new world, a new earth and a new Man. Our thoughts are not thought the way they were before the world began orbiting; our blood follows different paths. It is not the same vault of heaven shining above us; it is not the same sun standing above our heads; it is not the same night that wraps us in a cloak of darkness. It is not the same time speeding by, for it is the planets that speed. Is it the same death we die?

No wonder that Galileo was martyred! Or that they who said 'But it does move' were tortured as the world's greatest rebels and heretics.

It was 'a new evening and a new morning' from that same hour.

*

How beautiful the old world order was.

In the deep blue of the heaven the naiades lay at peace by the brooks, drinking in the splendour of the sun, earth's glorious candelabrum - the sun which did not go hurtling on through infinite space but rose up from the earth's own sea and slowly described his arc over noon and on to evening and again laid himself to rest in the earth's sea, whilst night stepped forth with all its tiny candles. The earth itself lay at peace in the ocean where all dark mysteries swam, resting securely on its pillars at the four corners. And deep within the deep mysterious forest sat Pan, piping his four notes which were endlessly repeated as a whispering in the branches, as an echo from the hills, as a rippling in the brooks.

*

And now!

The brain's thought, the eye's vision, microscope, telescope, spectroscope, they have drawn back the curtain upon a design, a network, a mesh behind the mists of substance. Behind the muscles, behind the green leaf, behind the hard stone, in among cells, in among planets. A glorious design of curving, sweeping lines with radiant interspace.

Do you see it? Do you see the temple reaching out over all space, the tabernacle of the universe? Do you see the living firmaments, the lines entwining and embracing, speeding and intersecting, ever more remarkable, ever stranger.

Do you see?

Did you see how, even as you were looking, it changed! The tabernacle of the universe is vibrating! The columns are shuddering. The arches are shaking.

There is no standing still out there in the blue of space. It is a dance!

In that one second a new world plexus came into being! There was a new temple! A million lines became a million new ones! One of them might gently vibrate whilst a thousand others leap. The one might take a thousand years for its renewal, others a thousandth of a second.

Some cells change under combustion; some dance themselves to death. Every line contorts itself, every spiral incurvates itself!

You see! It happened that second! That second is a thousand years! That second is a million years!

Just look at those long straight threads linking member to member, those most visible to the human eye. Watch them, row upon myriad row of them, as they so faintly begin to tremble, so imperceptibly assert their will - creating the new, drawing new lines, twisting and turning. See, as the urgency grows, the strangely intricated play of those curving lines!

Or when they embrace and couple, seize hold of each other, cross each other, fusing two into one or from two forming thousands.

And the atoms! The molecules and the cells! In ranks, in clusters. Four and four, six and six, ten and ten. In motley hosts. Wave upon wave of vibrant images. Like swarms of gnats, each separately dancing whilst the whole swarm drifts soundlessly along. Like flocks of birds.

The very network of the universe!

Vibrating, seething, surging, bubbling, fermenting. Wanting the new, in a frenzy to create new worlds, new realms of beauty, new galaxies, and every minute there are new harmonies of lines, every second, every thousandth of a second, or every millenium until perhaps they stop and pause among the new cosmic images which emerged from that dance of life, the new tabernacles that tremble with life's astonishment, the astonishment of being!

The individual cells, the individual worlds - the swarms, the galaxies that comprise the individual elements, with each individual's brief temporal journey held within the great eternal journey - a speeding and a journeying and a changing of places!

Look! Look how it creeps, leaps, swims, flies! Look how it trembles, swerves, dances, speeds! Creatures and worlds! Atomic systems and planetary systems!

The tabernacle of the world lives! It dances!

The tabernacle of the world is transforming itself. At this very second! With this very breath!

*

Everywhere there is light. Light which refracts into colours. Colours which flicker and flame, live and die, refract anew, dance in rhythm with the living creatures and the worlds like veils in a dancer's hands.

Everywhere there is sound. Every step in the dance has its note. Just as here on earth there are sounds that sweep and surge, so too is it out there in endless space. To us it is silence. For out there different laws of sound prevail.

Perhaps the entire cosmos is playing a hymn of praise! Perhaps all existing things comprise the instruments of an orchestra which is playing the wedding march of Life!

*

At times I feel as though I am drawn close to all this. I am in the midst of cosmic sound, in the smithy of the universe. All about me there is a hustling and a bustling, a glowing and a pounding.

Indeed there are times when I seem to glimpse it within my own self. It is all happening within me. The whole loom of the world is vibrating within me.

And I am afraid. All turns black before my tightly shut eyes, and I scarcely dare breathe. It is as though death were drawing near. As though death breathed on me. Or life. The flaming fire on Mt Horeb which Moses was forbidden to approach too near.

Behind my closed eyes I see the motion of the heavenly bodies, sweeping along in that sea of colour which existed before the Creation. And I see colours of such incandescence as the human retina cannot bear to look upon, behind the plexus of cells, within it. For did not planets exist before Man was created? I see eternities within my brain, whole millenia which have passed, and I hear the echo of those millenia within the convolutions of my brain. And I see white-hot worlds tossed along in my blood, fiery masses sweeping along behind my own soul. I see worlds consumed by fire just to give birth to a single frisson in my soul.

And there can be nights when all is quiet outside, when the whole world is quiet and everything seems asleep - people and beasts and spirits and God himself - when something comes over me. I seem to sense a throbbing within me which is *not* within me, which dark eternities ago once was there but is now infinitely distant in space. And the thought runs through me: God does not sleep! At this very moment he is creating!

And I see the glowing heat within me. It is as though my vibrant spirit had walked among volcanos in the morning of time when solids were molten. Deep within me I see the forge of the universe, streaming, revolving, burning and hammering. I hear the hammer blows of creation -and I feel as though I too could surely create! Create! I am aware of a faint echo of pleasures humankind has never dreamed of, the joy of creating life! And that echo, merely that dim awareness, makes me stiffen with terror!

*

Everything out there is within me. My soul, my body emerged from the volcanic eruption of the worlds.

Strange to the point of terror: people rise from their beds, eat their meals, go to work, lie down to sleep, and they never hear it, never see it - this inner world.

I imagine all is quiet. I am not aware of anything moving in the room. Suddenly I feel my eyelids twitch. Nothing seems to be moving. I strain my attention, and suddenly I feel my scalp contract. What this means I do not know. And yet there is perhaps a long history behind it. Perhaps it is the product of a thousand impulses.

Things are at work within me. Everywhere - seething, boiling, burning, changing. I hear nothing. I remark nothing. It is totally still. A week from now and not even my muscles are the same. Yet it never occurs to me to remark it, for I am unaware of it.

I know that my blood is endlessly coursing, circulating, bubbling. I know because I have read such things. All this miraculous labyrinthine circulation of the blood. I have never seen it; never wish to see it; indeed *must* not see it. One day I might happen to cut my finger, and a shudder runs through me. My own blood! I look at the beautiful purple-red drops with something like terror, as though they were something alien which I am encountering suddenly and unexpectedly. But what can also happen - at a moment when all is silent about me - is that suddenly I hear something. Something beating.

The heart's beat. Gathered into one song, one single march, the legend of the thousand mysterious and inscrutable tremors of the body.

There must be many who have had that same strange feeling when in a silent hour they have felt these same heart beats. As something sacred, something beyond them, above them.

*

And the clock, ticking in the silent hours, can also bring on strange moods.

Is it because it resembles the heart? Is the heart a pendulum?

The one difference being that the clock, made by human hands, can be wound up again when it is run down.

The heart cannot be wound up when it is run down. That is death. Each heartbeat ticking away is one swing of the pendulum nearer death.

And when the heart is run down is there anyone who can make the human clock go again? Is there some great mechanic who knows better than men how to make machines, who made these clocks for the enrichment of the world and set them going and who can wind them up anew after they have stopped?

Perhaps after repair?

*

Is Death neither a man with a scythe nor a black-clad woman nor a white spectre? Is it a god - the only one - which is Death?

One who only once passes over a human life? In the hour when he gives up the ghost?

Is Life what we call God?

*

Yes. At one time things in the universe stood still. All was peace. Now all is movement, vibration, flux.

Here into my little room is carried from dawn till night a rushing sound as of a new Atlantic. It is of the electric trains which go speeding past carrying thousands of people, thousands of human hearts. When I go down there, the turmoil is such that it makes one ill to look at. All those things driven by steam and by gas and all the forces of the earth, running, chasing. Round a thousand pivotal points, round shops and markets, round banks where the banknotes soundlessly flow in and out in a never-ending flood. And at dusk I find myself walking past seas of flame where I see iron bars glowing, see huge pounding monsters who with one blow punch rows of round holes, see faces teeming and flaming in the smoke and naked labouring arms - such is life all around us, thus it roars in our brains. The brain is a glowing forge, everything is wheel and belt, a vibrating and a revolving. If it looks out into space, it no longer finds a broad, peaceful pearl-spangled tapestry, but instead a rushing and a wheeling in millions of orbits. Stars are born, planets vanish, comets plunge.

In the end one grows so weary of seeing it, of feeling it. It is as though all those hammers were hammering on the soft tissues of the brain. Confused, the thoughts sink down exhausted: Is there no longer any peace?

Could I but describe in words what I have sometimes felt within me! It was too immense for me to form any clear idea of it; yet the burning feeling coursed through me that could I but grasp the idea in it, it would

43

be like opening closed and secret doors to a sequestered sea of light, a forgotten - nay, an undiscovered - sea of light. I could only feel as though I were in the midst of that glowing rushing turmoil - that I had entered into some strange and lofty church, loftier than any church of stone, which thrust its spire far up into the maelstrom of the universe. And there everything was so still, so still - and yet, no! It was not still!

What was it? None of the words that run to my pen can say it. They are old and rusty. It was like an inward echo from distant space, making every cell of my body distend and fill with ether, turning every cell within me into a sphere of resonance, a mighty organ note making it seem as if an invisible church was vaulted over my soul. A mighty organ note so powerful as to raise me bodily and bear me aloft. An organ note - no! a sigh, a sigh as from a springtime wind of heaven, a drawing of breath.

A breath. A heartbeat of heaven!

I looked at the Great Bear, I looked at the Seven Stars and I surely thought that they stood there so peacefully, and that that was how they had stood for Aristotle and Plato. Then I seemed to feel something come over me from these worlds, from far beyond them. Rhythm? How often has one not spoken of the rhythm of space, of the rhythm of the universe. What is the use of words - for that something that passed through me was newer than any words!

Rhythm in all things! In the infinitely great as in the minutest of cells!

As he stands in front of all the various instruments, the conductor describes with his hand a little triangle or a square and it wings its way over violin and horn and drum; and it is part of every leaping bow-stroke, in every trilling run - the little triangle is part of all these, all these.

That is the way rhythm goes: in under the web of the universe, orbiting, spiralling, labyrinths of lines, the atoms and the worlds, they dance to it, they live by it: the axis, the basis, the line of the rock and of the crystal.

Every little world looks for the beat, or contains it within itself, perhaps without knowing. Its substance, its body feels the pull. They love. They love and they gather two by two, in groups, in harmonies. And in this there is repose, repose in all the movement and haste, equilibrium.

Rhythm - this is the peace of the new life of the universe. Rhythm is the peace of Life, of eternity perhaps. Immobility is that of Death.

I look at my dead words. And what I felt was perhaps a presentiment of Life, of God's breathing.

*

The entire life of the cosmos one tremendous song of praise! Planets, cells and living creatures all instruments in an orchestra playing the wedding march of Life!
Is there anyone to wield the baton?

*

A mundane little orchestra in a concert hall is already in itself a thing of wonder! Often as I sit watching it, watching all those moving bows and trembling strings, I forget to listen to the music. It is like a kind of enchantment: all these violins, all these flutes and horns rising in tiers up from the platform, all this host of sounding instruments - all there just to evoke some small vibration in my soul. This seems to belong to *my* age as nothing else does - this age in which I live and breathe and suffer. Is music not the art that came flowing from *our* hearts, from the hearts of those who have lived here on earth in modern times, these centuries of steam and railway as well as of the science of harmonics! It came along with the new vision of the universe; it was born along with Copernicus.

The art of the ancients was the art of stone. The art of leaping bows, of vibrating strings, of dancing columns of air is ours. We do not seek beauty in repose, in the fixed line. What we seek is the line before it is fixed, that which gave birth to the word and to the form, the metamorphosis which is more permanent than the substance. Even in stone, in sculpture, in arches and in vaultings we feel fluidity and undulation; and thoughts and words *sing* out from our brains.

And as I sit gazing at the orchestra playing, for me it is like looking into the whole workings of the universe. The slim glistening violin bows all in line, and in new ranks the silver-stopped flutes, and the shining horns and then the contrabasses - so different in appearance yet all intent on the one same thing: to join in, just to join in and follow the conductor's hand. And the drum. Behind it all the drum. The drum which is the heavy stalactite of rhythm itself, rhythm petrified, its very law of gravity. Yet sometimes it has the sound of dread, the confusion of the beating heart, or like the cloudbank's flurried disquiet. Or - and precisely because it is like the very law of rhythm - all things seem dark and menacing when there is disquiet among the drums. If they falter, it is like some impending collapse ... of the worlds.

And I look upon this and I seem to see spirits of creation dancing past me. Everything is working, working, working. Serene and complete, a painting confronts us. Here is a tumult of bows, myriads of hands, hosts of white human hands in the most various of movements, hosts of dancing human hands - visible thoughts, visible currents of the soul.

And behind it all and central to it, a little black baton. It writes strange runic characters. What do they mean? Are they signs writ in air of the alphabet of the human heartbeat? Is it the beat of the human heart which has resolved itself and burst forth in the thousand notes of violin and cello, oboe and trumpet?

*

And all these struggling, dancing fingers exist only for the sake of a little musical note. All they are there for is to produce a sound in the passages of my ear. All that cascade of movement!

All these long-haired men, all these white shirtfronts mean nothing to me. Not even this variety of instruments means anything. Twenty violins are there to produce one stroke, and the more it is *one* the better.

Perhaps it would be best if a canopy were to be placed over them all. Invisible like the soul itself, the harmony would come lilting and fill the air about me with splendour. Why do I have to know about all those restless hands, about all these people working by the sweat of their brows?

But if we could arrange it thus, would we? No! We like it as it is. We *want* to see the hands behind the music. We *want* to see the strange encounter of the baton and the swirling rhythms and the banks of strings.

We actually want to see the sweat on the faces. We find a personal pleasure in this. A 'modern' pleasure. Seeing the melodies emerging, pure and proud, the product of the assembled hands. We love to see the music as it is being made, to see the birth of sound.

*

The curtain is drawn back from the tabernacle of the universe. We see the instruments of the universe playing. We see the forces of nature vibrating. With their probes, their lenses and their scalpels, our researchers penetrate to the very basis of things. And what at one time had perhaps appeared to some brooding spirit as a kind of fairy-tale vision is now brought into the full light of day. We have reached the ocean floor of natural forces; we have insinuated ourselves into the inner centre of matter; we were near the point of seeing how life itself was formed, when it grew dark for us there on the ocean floor. Things closed in upon us, and we shuddered. We were like fledgling birds wanting to be out into the wide sky - but, alas, we lacked something at the roots of our wings.

The orchestra is too big for us. And we sit within it. We do not make the connections. The instruments are too near to us. There is a fermenting and a seething and a roaring, and we see neither the beginning nor the end of things. Our hearts turn faint.

And the question is asked: *Is* there a baton?

If there is one, it is infinitely far away. We see things turning over as though they were turning of their own accord.

And perhaps there is no overall baton. He who composed the orchestra's music - if indeed anybody did - is surely much too dignified to show his baton.

He set it in motion. And he said: 'See what I have done! Is not everything exceeding good?'

Perhaps in the end it is the commandment we should see, this matter of life and death. Not only see, but feel in our inmost hearts how exceeding good it was. And feel within us terror and reverence and cast ourselves down on our knees and forget our own little selves, because our own selves found in the great Life about us a Self so jubilant and so mightily splendid that we trembled with ecstasy if we could but sense within us the faintest trace of that great Self.

- We have begun to see the instruments of that universal orchestra, but we have only just begun. And all around us there is still an ear-splitting noise. It is not yet music to our ears. We have not distanced ourselves enough yet. We are not high enough yet in the great blue vault.

Will it take centuries yet before it makes complete music to the minds of men?

*

Yes, there were moments when I felt as though a temple was rising above me from out of the centre of the maelstrom, and as though the whirling dance was turning to music.

Once again the stars were there above me as they were when I was a little child, clear, peaceful. As they were for Aristotle, for Plato.

And yet not the same. The blue star-filled heaven was not dead. It was filled with heat. It was alive as I was. The planets and the cells all circled and sped but with composure, rising and falling in rhythm with something even deeper in the cosmos, rising and falling as my heart rose and fell.

The space about me was alive. It was filled - with spirit! It hummed with activity among all the heavenly bodies, but gently. Not with a consuming flame but a fragrant warmth.

I felt the approach of something that enveloped my soul, something that swooped on powerful swan's wings in and among the stars. And I felt I must sink to my knees in great fear. I dared not look up into the vault of the universe, but had to shut my eyes. And I shut my eyes, and through my body there surged this rhythm of the universe, not confused and disturbing but in an ecstatic universal embrace. It ran down my spine. I felt I was being forced to my knees, yet I dared not bend the knee! For...

It ran down my spine and into the many chambers of my body. And it seemed as though life - true life - might then, that very instant, begin.

All things, inner and outer, were in radiant order within that mighty compelling rhythm - with one thing rising that another might fall.

Yes, in all those millions there was one inspiring plan, and the most distant was linked to the most inward by vibrant strings. Strings stretched from the most distant and largest planet to the minutest, most inward cell. The least hair of my head had its place in this incommensurable plan, was a part of it.

But how can words express what is greater than words? Words are Man's invention, a product of his brain. Yet all this was greater even than Man and Man's mind. A symphony might convey some faint idea of it. For if, in some rare moment, the world reveals its music to a human soul, there is no seeing any longer but a hearing. The perception is no longer by thought and brain but by the whole body's resonance, on its nerves and in its blood. No longer something visual, but something else.

It may be that in that moment when, by some happy chance, the soul catches a faint strain of the music in the tabernacle, it *must* vibrate. It cannot do otherwise. For it is itself caught up in the rhythm, and can do no other.

Therefore all my words are halted. The great Sublime, the Glory, the world of serene movement, the world of rhythmic breathing - again and again I try to bring things back to words, and I cannot.

*

The world revealed itself to humankind. New continents emerged in distant oceans; new planets with new creatures coursed above the people's heads; new beasts extended their claws in the wildernesses of the Orient; new peoples with different faces and of different colours emerged from the world's teeming multitudes; new peoples with new gods. The world opened up its abundance. No longer was there any need for the monsters of mythology, or for the fantastic plant growths of the fairy-tale. The primeval forests were full of them. From the warm ocean beds strange creatures stretched out their tentacles. Not even the smallest plot of land in the whole wide world remained silent. Every corner lived and breathed and stretched forth feeling hands. The microscope traced an infinity of tiny worlds in which monsters in reverse swam and crawled and flew. Not a single speck of matter was still. Everywhere there was a breathing and a moving.

And the speed in the human brain increased. It was as if new convolutions were needed there to cope with the proliferation of new images and concepts and all the new combinations which had been created. Peace had disappeared from the earth and from the brain; the railways blew their whistles; and steel wires darkened the clear air. Wilder and wilder grew the dance.

But see!

Slowly there emerged from the turmoil a dream, the dream of rhythm.

From the very turmoil itself it came, more urgently than ever before in time.

From the silent chambers where the night lamp burned among alembic and beaker, where the enquiring human mind kept watch whilst the rest of mankind slumbered red-cheeked among the bolsters there came something like a mystic legend: there is a oneness in heat, in sound, in light and in electricity. One common thing: and that is rhythm, unique, endlessly shifting, endlessly vibrating.

A flood of blinding light then invaded the realms of the brain, as though an electric light had been lit in the kingdom of the spirit, as though steam had been raised to fuel the driving thoughts.

Look! Just when it seemed that the horizons were darkening, that walls would imprison the soul in unending turmoil, more paths than ever leading to unity and clarity seemed to open up. Could it really be that now was the time - this age of the sphere, the decimal, the circle - when the way would lead to the centre of things more readily than in the age of astrological numbers, the age of forest nymphs and satyrs, the age of multiple gods? Could this be possible?

Already from these silent chambers, from these sacristies of human enquiry, there reaches us a whisper that fills us with astonishment and mighty foreboding:

That age-old dream - that dream which a child's innocent brain perhaps retains from the mystery of birth and which the childlike brains of the great philosophers have re-discovered - is true. There is but one thing. There is but one substance, and energy is its soul.

Look!

More and more clearly the people are acknowledging one truth that flames through body and soul: if there is a god then there is but one.

Yes, it has come thus far: that the human brain can no longer comprehend more than one. The human heart can no longer be drawn to more than one.

One. Greater than all the many together. One. Of which all the others from the great spirit of the forest to the synod's Holy Ghost were mere abstractions. One because God can only be one, because the human heart and brain cannot conceive God as other than one.

And only now perhaps has the age arrived when the people, in truth and with all their soul and all their body, can rejoice and shout: 'The Lord our God, the Lord is one.'

For many days, a week and more, I was filled with thoughts and visions. I felt as though the universe had opened up to me and that all things had become one in a flood of light.

Tonight it was all overturned.

I had written the last line. Had put out the light. Was already asleep.

Then it happened. I woke. I shot up. I shuddered from head to foot. There was something in the room. As yet I could not see anything. But I felt there was something. I sat up in bed. A broad band of moonlight fell across the floor. I looked around. I looked at all the things in my room. Ah, it seemed to me I saw them that night as I had not seen them for a long time - more precisely, each separate thing. Had the sun just fogged them?

I cannot describe what passed through me at the realization that there was something in the room - some living thing, something besides me that was alive.

Suddenly I saw it. It crossed the band of moonlight. It crept soundlessly away in the silence of the night, soundless, black.

It was a rat.

Nothing more than a rat. But a thousand thoughts ran down my spine, as I sat there cold and shivering. How did *it* figure in the rhythm of things, this rat? In this universe with its lilting song and its coursing planets and its cells in suspension? What was it doing there with those eyes in the dark and its little disgusting tail?

It lived and had its being; it belonged. It presumably had feelings, was conscious of my presence in the world. So what had this thing to do with my soul? And what had my soul to do with it?

It was there. It was in my world. If I held it a few inches in front of my eyes it would blot out all the suns and the whole of space.

*

And I remembered another night that had brought cold sweat to my back.

I had lain there unable to sleep. Lashed by my thoughts. Thoughts which seemed to be not only in my brain but in my body, in my flesh, as though they lay stinking in my entrails. I felt the whole room was stinking. I ridiculed the idea and battled against it.

But at last I had to put on the light.

And there on my pillow I saw a great, swollen, flat bed-bug.

*

51

Possibly from some point of view it might be possible to see the rat and the bed-bug as beautiful.

I can never do that. I shudder all over when I see the flat body of a bug, and the stench from it seems to darken all that is light within me.

So is there a world wholly hostile to mankind?

The Middle Ages conceived the world as being peopled by an army of dark beings, devils, trolls, evil spirits.

But the bug that lives in the beds of electrically lit Paris hotels and crawls across the violently trembling nerves of persecuted modern man - what is it doing?

Why should it exist? What is it doing in the world? Where did it come from? How did it enter the creative imagination of an all-powerful God? What is this God like who willed it into existence? Is *he* created in man's image?

*

Is then the life of these worlds not a dance, not a song of praise, but a battle for life and death between two realms? Is there a world of darkness?

*

When I recall the stench of the bug, I begin to understand this word 'sin'. Perhaps it is in the world, this thing. Perhaps it fills the whole globe with a stench we do not comprehend because we are not used to things being any different. We walk in a darkness we call light; occasionally it might seem to the more sensitive among us that there is something heavy in the air, something that does not smell very nice. The young man who has only just left behind the sunlit life of childhood finds his mind overlaid by a terrible melancholy because the things he sees about him are not as beautiful and fair as the things his infant soul lived among and longed for. This melancholy is called *Weltschmerz*. And people laugh at it. But perhaps it has something to do with the celestial bodies. Perhaps it is that the instinct which led the hands of the children to the violets will never return.

Yes, we might sometimes feel that there is something heavy in the air, something which does not smell as sweet as the roses. We cannot light a lamp, or then we might see great flat bugs crawling about.

*

People have things within them they do not want to touch.

The cosmic spirit and the excreta!

Can the earth be a home to humans so long as it is thus with them?

Is the world anything more than a gigantic midden where men and beasts endlessly and incessantly pour out their impurities?

*

These last few evenings I have been sitting in the company of some poor and sick people. They tell me their stories: day after day in toil and slavery, in hunger, sickness in their bones, disappointed in their hopes.

As the flickering rays of the candle fall on those wasted features, the eternal question recurs again and again:

Why must mankind suffer this - mankind whose thoughts can soar to the sun, mankind who has built churches the thousand lofty vaults of which reach up towards the brilliant light, mankind who conquered the tiger and defeated the leviathan - why is his back bent down to the ground, why does he drag his feet in the dust, why are the lines of his face contorted in ugliness?

Yet sometimes I have seen a look in an old person's eyes, a look that sought the window and far beyond, a look that spoke of something which yearned for fiery splendour.

And as I walked down the dark stairs, I murmured: 'The majesty of humankind!'

*

The room where the old man lies is dark and gloomy. The candle flickers in the draught from the window where some of the panes have old newspaper instead of glass.

Outside the sky is beautiful, like a blue cloth embroidered with pearls. The stars form delightful patterns.

Under this sky man was born naked. It is told that he woke to life among flowers and gentle beasts and sweet fruits. With his beautiful limbs he sprawled in the soft grass amid the intoxicating scent of roses.

Now man lies on a wooden bed in straw jumping with fleas. He lies between rough blankets crawling with lice.

Not even the bird of the air nor the beast of the field lies so hard, breathes so heavily, eats so miserably as this white-haired son of the earth who toiled year after year, three hundred and sixty five toil-weary days in each.

*

Yet what am I saying?

Humankind swathes its body in silk and stretches out its ample limbs on down plucked from the eider duck's warm breast.

It collects the fragrance of the flower in crystal bottles and with it bathes its hair that this hair might smell like the rose of the forest. And because its skin is not white enough for its delight it dusts white powder on its face. And because its lips are not red enough it paints them with costly salves.

And when it rises and walks it glides over soft carpets, walking over those carpets with slow proud steps like a god.

And it takes its food from silver dishes and arranges beautiful flowers among those steaming dishes and sets out all the splendours of nature on the dazzling white cloth and fills the carafes with red and golden wines; and on the fingers that hold the polished goblets are rings that glitter with jewels and gold, brilliant with all the colours of the rainbow.

But then mankind began to build great towns and assemble all the people in great blocks of dwellings.

In these great halls there is a radiance of crystal and purple and silk. But above and below, in attic and in cellar, there is sighing day and night.

And when all the people have been stuffed into these boxes, will a lament resound across the earth, will poisonous fumes rise from the chimneys up to heaven, and finally will a sickness slink into the hearts of those with the white hands?

*

Do they then drink the wine that dances in the blood in order that they might forget?

How can they drink it with pleasure when mankind has become lower than the lowest creature that crawls upon the earth?

Has humankind no pride?

When from their great halls they ride to church in their gilded carriages, psalm-book in hand, passing the narrow streets where they see old men, their faces gaunt from toil and grief, coming to the cellar door to catch a glimpse of the Sunday sun, not daring in their wretched rags to approach 'God's House' - are they not ashamed?

Mankind whose thoughts go storming towards the light, whose optical instruments take him up among the stars - is he not able to clothe his nearest neighbour decently?

*

I have read of islands in the Pacific which have seen nothing of Sodom and Babylon, and which have not been caught up by the terrible cogwheels of 'work'.

Those who live there are like children. They are happy.

When the moon shines they sit together and breathe the warm fragrance of the night. Roses and fruits do not grow in vain. The moon does not shine in vain.

And the dream that comes from earth and sea and sky takes possession of them, carries them away, enflames their bodies, and they dance among the green of nature - dance dances which existed before man's brain grew old, their naked bodies swaying in exultation, wilder and ever wilder in fevered excitement, lifting garlands of flowers high towards the vault of heaven.

They are like children. And we are like adults. No longer do we run, drunk with joy, towards the blue and yellow flowers of the field. We imagine that only after we had been torn away from the earth and had begun to move forward in endless procession did we have the right to bear the proud name: princes of the world.

Well, it must surely be one of the greatest wonders of the world that we with our brilliant ideas, our range of feeling and our strangely compounded passions still are linked to those living on those islands.

Yet it is melancholic to sit here amidst the factory smoke and think of them. For they are happy. And we are not. The higher it grew -this mighty tree of civilization of which we are so proud - the unhappier we became. Will it always continue thus?

And when we arrived at the thing which was to make the world richer than anyone had dreamed - the machine - things became worse than ever. We created something that made otiose all the old images of hell. Civilization created something that did not exist in nature, nor even in the imagination: London!

Man, create a London without its Whitechapel and then praise thyself!

But as long as Whitechapel is with us should we not all go in mourning?

Did I not see in the eye of my old man a look that spoke of a yearning for beauty and grandeur? A look that said there is nobody - not even the meanest person in the blackest hovel - who was not born with the same spark of nobility within him as the noblest prince.

But the 'savage' out on the islands in the sea is nobler than that poor man living where culture is at its densest. For he dances a dance to beauty, and his soul dreams.

*

On the stairs in one of these poverty-stricken houses I met an old school friend who is a doctor. We had a long talk together. There was an openness about him, but different from my brother clergymen.

'Away with your heaven!' he cried. 'Bring your heaven down to earth. Make a heaven on earth. Is that not a good enough religion? Oh, if only I could!' And he shook his fist against an invisible something.

'All this talk of the transcendental, of the invisible, of the after-life. Always it gets in the way of honest human endeavour. Is it not this that ties our hands? These hands of ours in which the power of the earth flourishes.

'They think about angels, and they have no time for cultivating the fields of the Lord! They think about angels, and they forget their own blue-eyed children!

'Heaven and hell - these are the worst enemies of the human will. Do we have time to think about China when our own country is in danger? Have we time to think about hell' - his eyes glittered - 'so long as we have *that* up there in those houses?'

I remonstrated that a hope of heaven was the one comfort those people up there had, the one light in their darkness.

'Comfort! They don't need comfort! What they need is stirring up! They should be taught to see their wretchedness! See it and feel bitter! So that millions of grimy hands reach out. Demanding! And accusing! Accusing those who lulled man's will to sleep! Those who fragmented and enfeebled our splendid powers!

'Have we not imagination enough to picture an Eden here below, here on earth, in our midst?

'Oh, when I think of all the things mankind disposes over: those brilliant abilities we possess, this coursing life's blood, these powers we have to build and to form, these soaring ideas which we then consolidate with our hands, this fount from which to draw new beauties from our souls and brains, new and again new, richer than all we see around us, sublimer even than those of Nature! And when I think that all this is withering away, is dying, being scattered to the winds!

'Imagine if all this were to be concentrated! What are people not capable of when they are united, where they walk shoulder to shoulder, where all are ready to act as one, as a single new individual with their strength, their brilliance, their imagination multiplied a millionfold!

'Do we not have that responsibility? The churches speak of "sin". Is there any greater sin than this waste? Whichever way all the splendour we see around us and within us came into being, whether it was created by a god in human likeness or whether it evolved over thousands of years, is it not a sin against the earth we sprang from to let it decay? A sin against the sun that fills it like a beaker brimful with fecundity? A sin against the laws of the universe whose harmony is preached by night and by day? A sin against that which is even more distant and remote and behind it all?

'No, as long as there is still be found any man who has not become as a prince, has not the sun in his thoughts and pride in his eyes, then we still have use for our heads and our hearts and our hands. And we can let the angels sleep in peace.

'Would that not be a religion which would touch with warmth the hearts of humankind?

'But like other religions it demands faith! People will readily believe in an Eden somewhere out in space. But talk to them about an Eden here on earth! If only they had faith, even no larger than a mustard seed!'

And when we had taken leave of each other and had turned to go our separate ways, he cried after me: 'I have faith!'

And his eyes shone as one who has a faith he would die for. Die, not by an hour of martyrdom but by the burden of a lifetime's endeavour.

*

This haunted me all day long. Not so much his words - how often had I not wrestled with these ideas! - as his face and his eyes as he spoke.

He had faith. It was gospel for him.

That day has remained in my memory as I wandered about in the early morning and saw people hurrying to factory and workshop and office, all those striding, confident and happy people, each to his work. I remember the feeling I had, more oppressive than ever before, of being outside, of not belonging, like someone who hides himself and flees, branded.

If only I could be a part of it! If only I could accept the faith that shone in his eyes, and lose myself in it! I am a priest after all. I too could achieve something. For the word has power. It can comfort, soothe, give courage, inspire strength. I could go among them, gather them about me, comfort the weary, inspire the faint-hearted, proclaim the new gospel, have faith in their work, faith in a future when that work will have borne fruit a thousandfold and thus won nobility and respect.

*

And a great vision unfolded before me: a new Ignatius!

A new Jesuit order with its purpose on earth and not in heaven.

Why shouldn't that be possible? Why shouldn't one follow the call of the spirit when it flames and leave home and possessions in order to take a wonderful and splendid possession of the sacred idea!

To call together brothers, apostles, and send them out to preach and speak and work, each one in his own field. To put words on their lips, kindle fire in their souls - fire catches, fire spreads - to ignite other souls. A new-born fanaticism would sustain the task. The thought of helping to create a new force in the world would bring joy and delight. They would preach in chapel and in theatre; they would make their appearance in church and in workplace, in the marketplace and in the park, everywhere. Not with flags and drums and the blare of music. No, with a gleam in the eye and words on their lips, things which ultimately reach much further than sound and fury. Words straight out of the vibrancy of the age. Words for deprived and aching minds. They would boldly and unreservedly proclaim their earthly aims and their earthly faith, not seeking to recruit soldiers for some Samaritan army by offering heavenly rewards, not buying earthly credit with promissory notes on heaven. Would that not get further than the confused message of the Salvation Army?

Like the Jesuits of old they would infiltrate everywhere, force their way in everywhere: into schools, into offices, into the government. The new gospel would have to spread into newspapers, into parliaments, and there bring to white-hot heat what was cold and rational and create a vigorous resolve in place of fruitless partisan debate.

People of course work in this world. And they discuss, and they write. And here and there a person might sit in silence and brood about the solution to society's problems. But what would the ideas of one person achieve? Work is what changes the face of life. The work of countless hands.

Suppose the cry went forth everywhere! Suppose it became a religion for young people beginning their lives and their jobs! Suppose it became the first, great, consuming demand: that all minds must come together to determine the plan of work, and then all hands carry it out!

Suppose our present luke-warm ballot-box skirmishes were to become instead a religion that flamed in hearts and minds, would we not achieve in a single year what now takes centuries! And would not the chaos of human life be resolved, and brilliant light be thrown upon humanity's path!

*

I sat there seeing the whole plan in my mind's eye right down to its last details until my brain sagged with weariness.

Then suddenly I felt as I did that day when I walked down by the ships: It was like a hand on the back of my neck - and I froze.

I had felt so indescribably enthusiastic, thinking about those things. It seemed as though a thousand new vital forces were about to come to life within me. I too could have something to live for.

Then everything grew desolate. I looked up and out. I saw that the heavens *were* theie. I saw that there were millions of worlds.

They *were* there, the heavens. Stretching way over our heads, making our food with their sun. The red and yellow and blue of the flowers were simply a reflection of their rainbow.

Yes, within our own thoughts the very basis of thought was infinity - infinity in geometric series.

How can we distance ourselves from what is above us, what is behind us, what is within us?

*

Wouldn't those people I would preach to come at once to me and ask: 'But what about death? What use is all that to us if we do not know our own selves?'

The people in their palaces have all that earth can offer. All they have to do is stretch out their hands and all the splendours of the world come into their embrace. Are they happy? We know they are not. We know that sickness lurks among them in their minds and bodies. And even if all sickness were eradicated, would there not remain one thing to consume them, feeding on the roots of their hearts and the tips of their lungs -sin? Sin and dread? Dread, dread.

And I would have no answer.

*

I sat trying to picture to myself that great image: a victorious humanity, that new and glorious life on earth.

All at once a pair of eyes appeared before me. Whose were they?

As they manifested themselves more clearly I saw they were that poor old man's.

They turned to the window, looking beyond. Further and ever further.

And like a flash of pain the thought struck me: What were all those new and glorious things of one's dreams in comparison with this strange searching look born of the darkness of misery?

*

I have thought. I have seen great visions.

But the question keeps recurring: This being who is like me or unlike me - where is he, what does he want, what is he like, and how can I embrace him with all the ardour of my soul?

Christ I do not know. I try to embrace the great one, the unique one, but when I think I am near everything disappears in the mists about my heart. That lonely heart I hear beating, alone.

I can think no more. All is dark about my soul.

*

Why all this white heat within me - heat that seems to want to burn my pores to ashes?

60

If there is no-one to love! If with all my mind and body and soul I cannot enfold with a million arms some other being more splendid than me? Yes, there are days in the sun and nights in the dark when I feel as though every part of my body - its cells and the very souls of those cells - were stretching out millions of ardent arms. But they find nothing. And they sink down. Why is there this white heat within me? For me it is simply hell's torment.

*

How am I supposed to be able to love this Jehovah or this God the Father or this Christ or this Buddha? Not to speak of the 'Holy Ghost'.

It is not they who ignite the gathered threads of my being. For me they are as 'strange gods'. Demi-gods.

*

Do I believe in a god?

I do not know. But since this terrible conflict began in my soul, I have at least realized one thing: that I knew no god before. It has been a chaos of confusion, a collection of fragments and symbols filtered through the minds of the most variously constituted individuals at widely different ages and resulting in an adulterated mixture of book learning and inspiration.

I have seen much splendour these last few weeks, and sensed portents of great glory. I felt I was seeing the very laws of the universe themselves, throbbing, living, working. There was even one moving moment when I seemed to feel a spirit from beyond impinge upon my spirit.

But there were also times when everything grew cold, so cold. What help could be expected from that universal and infinite harmony for my poor little insignificant human body? For I could not address it as 'thou', nor take hold of a warm hand nor look into eyes in which was mirrored that small, insignificant, wonderful thing which is neither law of nature nor material splendour nor the wonder of rhythm but which we love.

*

It is afternoon. The sun is turning my room into a kingdom of light. It is playing on the spines of my books, turning them to living gold.

Who could believe, seeing my room at this moment, that it was not the very kingdom of peace?

Alas! What peace!

*

There is something in here apart from myself which is breathing. My camellia. It often seems like a living being to me. I can take it by one of its stems and feel it as though I were holding a woman's soft hand. Sometimes I have talked to it as though to a person. Why have I felt better for that? Does it answer - in the sense that its answer is transmuted into something I have no knowledge of but which finds its way secretly within me and works there to good effect?

*

Yes, my room looks like peace itself. Yet there is something here which is never at rest, which is in endless agitation like a pendulum or like the waters of the sea, now still, now rising: thought.

And thought murmurs in my ear: there is more than your camellia alive in here. Have you forgotten? I look. And there in the shaft of sunlight I see a dancing world of creatures I know nothing of.

And the thought persists and cries out: 'Every inch of this room is alive!'

I start up in dread: All these worlds! Are they friendly or hostile?

*

How can anyone imagine it is good to think there is no god?

How can anybody want to overlook the mightiest concept of all: the Creation?

The simple fact that this multitudinous miracle of microcosm and macrocosm even exists is enormous; even more tremendous is the profounder fact that all these things that live and have their being once came into existence.

Still greater is the thought of One creating these forms in advance and by some miraculous power of will being able to make them manifest.

But who will not imagine what is greatest?

And is not the greatest that which must be the truth?

*

62

Indeed the One who could conceive and create the seeds of life must be the most glorious being we can envisage. But the mere fact that our minds can formulate the thought - this idea that somebody was able to conceive and create the seeds of life before they existed - must surely compel us to hold fast to this idea if only because it is so miraculously radiant?

*

A new thing was born for me in that shaft of sunlight. I must get away. To the mountains.

Who knows whether in this confused swarm of ideas - this swarm which often merely drifts back and forth instead of working purposefully onwards and upwards - there may not be some small point waiting to manifest itself and bring order to this myriad play of light. Some small nucleus.

If I were to leave this room behind where my own old thoughts rattle against the walls of my brain and I were to quit this town and these streets where all is tradition and the remnants of a thousand years confront one, where the old petrified concepts stare down from every house wall and church window - if I were go up where there is eternal silence and eternal freedom and no human word is writ, I wonder if I might not find the focal point within myself?

I will go up into the mountains. I will see him. I will see God. Why should that not be possible? Millions of arms reach out from every atom of my being. I must have peace. I must live or die. I must seize hold of him. I will find him. I *will* see him.

I have been up there.

How can I describe it? I have been ill. For days I have lain as in a coma not daring to think. I feared for my sanity.

It must not collapse! That must not happen! Not yet!

What was it? Am I to believe it? Was it He?

All I know is that I went down on my knees. I had to. And I said the Lord's Prayer. So loudly that I heard the words passing over the waste land like some strange incantation.

All I know is that I shouted into the wind and the thunder as though my lungs would burst: 'What must I do?' And I listened for the answer, listened in the wind of heaven and in the waters of the earth and in the voice of the thunder.

And one thing I know: that away over the whole wide waste land I heard the sound of that age-old name echoing about my ears and my soul and my heart, and I thought it was death.

Jahveh.

*

I had walked a day and a night, and the next day came and it grew wilder and wilder. Nothing but deep black tarns with ice-cold rocks all around and snowfields and the endless army of boulders on the flat granite plain where the wind blows as it has always blown for hundreds and thousands of years.

I no longer walked, I ran. The howling wind threatened my mouth and my nose in a language older than the world itself. There was something mortally menacing there, something in the air, in the wind. But I was seized with the will to fight to the last fibre of my being.

Blizzards of snow and hail were flung against me to throw me to the ground. But though I had had no food for two days I raised up my arms and shouted: 'You will not have me!' And joyously I hurled myself against the driving snow, with a joy than ran as tears down my face melting the snow-flakes.

I saw the heavy dark clouds which had been gathering by the hour and covering more and more of the sky and enveloping all the peaks. Often I was near the point of throwing myself to the ground and giving up the struggle; and with my face to the ground to await my punishment if punishment there were to be. Or by my humility to avert the terror.

In the end I flung myself prostrate in the wet moss. But when I had rested but a minute on the soft earth, the thought took hold of me: Thunder and lightning and storm are but the order of nature. How else could I understand what the invisible powers wanted of me? If there indeed existed a spirit akin to - though much greater than - mine which wanted to communicate with me from out of the cloud, could he expect me to interpret a language I had never learnt?

And I leapt up and I laughed a ringing laugh, as loud as I could so that all might hear it - the wind and the cloud and the rocks. But the rocks returned my laughter - laughing in a way that sent glaciers down my back.

Hardly had the echo died away when there came a sound which was the most powerful and the most terrible I had ever heard in my life. It reverberated among the mountain peaks and shrieked through the air and over the earth and the lightning flashed so that I had to stop and shut my eyes. For immediately the old adage came to me: 'Never look at lightning!' And I thought perhaps there is some truth in that. And I dared not look at the lightning.

In mortal dread I counted the seconds between the lightning and the thunder and I realized it was still some distance away. And I told myself: It is only the forces of nature manifesting themselves up here in all their majesty. For if the storm had been menacing me it would have responded at once to my mocking laughter.

Yet breathlessly I waited to see if the lightning was approaching. Yes, the next flash showed it was closer. Whereupon I cried out in the direction of the lightning flash: 'Are you playing the fool with me?'

That same moment I flung myself to the ground for I distinctly heard within the thunder's roll : Jahveh! Jahveh!

I lay flat with my face to the ground and I shut my eyes and tried to shut all the other eyes in my body too. For above me there stood a being - whom I must not see for to see him is death - and flames shot criss-crossing through my brain, my arms, my bowels, my bones.

The whole thing lasted an eternity, lasted a second. But in it there was a brief moment when an excruciating pain passed through both my hands and both my feet. It felt as though a burning foot was stamping on each of them.

*

When I now think of it, I believe there was a period when I lost consciousness and it seemed as if my whole body was struggling against death.

I lost my breath, then breath was forced into me. And that breath held the sound of the name and in all the vaulted spaces there was only that one name.

But never can it be put into words. Death and life, that terrifying and that painful creation together in that one name, in the breathing spirit of that name - no, it cannot be deciphered by human words.

Nor was this name Jahveh. So turbulent a name, like the sound of death or life itself, does not belong to any earthly language. I know of only one word to reproduce it. But the name I heard cannot be repeated either by mouth or pen.

*

I am calm now. I have told myself that the whole thing was nerves. In all that incommensurable solitude, in that terrifying storm, your visions took on flesh and blood - visions that lie held in the brain from the time of your forefathers, from medieval times indeed.

Yet it was a great and fearsome thing. I shall never forget it. I remember it with all my body.

And one thing remains.

If those terrible inner storms and those glowing visions were in fact not reality, were not called into existence from above or from without but emerged from the dark labyrinth of my own inner being can there then be anything more mysterious in the whole compass of our thoughts and dreams and visions and imaginings than this convoluted thing we call the Self?

Is it not the greatest miracle of all that from the secret recesses of this Self there can be drawn storms and emotions and pains and dramas more than all our ordinary everyday life taken together - which *are* life, which to our souls and feelings are more real than any other form of life - which indeed *are* life and death and the ultimate.

But if this earthbound Self of ours has such wealth within itself, what must a Self of even more delicate, more audacious, more paradoxical and more multifarious reticulation be like?

And then one raised to a still higher power.

And yet again?

*

The storm abated. I rose and went. For a day and a half I had not seen a living soul. And more and more my brain began dividing things into those that stay still and those that move. Often I had to halt. Was that not something moving over there?

Towards evening I saw silhouetted against the sky in the distance a black shape which was moving. Yes, it *was* moving. It did not remain still. I halted and caught my breath. It was as if my blood had been thirty-seven degrees below freezing point and in an instant became thirty-seven above. I hurried on, trembling.

It was a lamb. I sat down and took it on my lap. It struck me that I had not touched an animal for a very long time, for years perhaps. I looked into its big, bright and strangely sad eyes. And I thought to myself: Is there not one and the same spiritual tide running through everything that lives and moves on this earth of ours?

And I pressed its lovely warm fleece against my breast which had been lashed by the wind. I pressed the lamb close to me and kissed it fervently on its snout.

Whereupon it bleated and looked at me with eyes full of terror. As though I were a dangerous enemy.

Those great sad eyes! They were like some mute unending lament at the divorce that exists between souls.

*

But as I let the lamb go and got up I experienced something so wondrous that I forgot everything.

The whole sky was full of roses. Below them, far distant, was a streak of soft light: the sea. But in among the reds and the pinks and all the other roses was one great fiery bloom, firmer and fuller than all the other roses strewn about the heavens in quiet profusion. That bloom was the sun.

And this sun looked me straight in the eyes, mild, friendly, with a smile like that of a mother who stands serene and utterly composed with her children at her full, heavy breasts and who is thus well able to smile a smile of beatitude to you.

There was no haste. Everything had time. She stood there smiling as though the world in *no* sense had begun to grow old, as though that evening was no different from the first primeval morning of creation. The way she stood there was as though it would all last for ever.

Slowly, gently, easefully the sun went down as it continued to look upon me. For it *did* look on me - on me who who had come there from the darkness of the mountain peaks.

And one sensed that it would continue beyond and behind the sea in the same delightfully calm way. And one felt that all the other suns were following their courses not in some restless impetuous way but with composed and serene majesty.

*

And thus I thought the sun did speak:

I am greater than the dark thundercloud, and my glorious rotundity is greater than the savage jagged rocks. Your spirit seeks what is steep, fearsome, dark. You think you will find the greatest power there. But the dark is *one*. In my light there is infinity.

Little mortal being, you can never get away from the one idea of God as power, as something able to destroy you. You saw the lightning flash, and you thought you felt the ineffable as never before. But the lightning is pointed, I am round. You think your God seeks you out in the dark under lowering clouds. Dear little mortal, don't you see now that the most powerful thing is the world is beauty? Beauty!

And, strange little mortal, could you not see that a god who sought you as I did, clad in a garment of roses and with a radiant smile on its countenance, was greater than the spirit that crushes your delicate nerves like an avalanche?

True, he is terrible in his might, this god. Even I am fire. But oh! he is more! He is an infinity of light compared to the one of the lightning flash.

But you have lost yourself in abstractions. All your truths are abstractions and therefore dead - all your gods.

Yes, I look down on your earth and see that what you have done is well conceived. I see all your machines and find them remarkable. But, mortal, do you not see that the whole network of machines encompassing your earth is a grinning skeleton?

Skeletons, abstractions.

Your machines, your laws, your systems, what are they all compared to the woman standing in the warmth and light of the sun letting the milk flow from her full breasts to those rose-red lips.

See these breasts - they are as I am, they are worlds. Roses are bursting suns. Yes, the most beautiful things known to your eye on earth are created in my image and its.

All those great philosophers and men of learning who took your breath away - what were they all for? And your governments and the work of millions of hands - what were they for? What was the point of it all? Was it not all so that she might stand there contentedly in the midst of it all, and that I might shine undisturbed on that white breast as the milk ran? And that she might be beautiful and the child beautiful?

Of all things known to your eye and your mind is there anything more powerful than that vision? Has any philosopher formulated anything greater than this: Life - in beauty?

Are not all words, all ideas, all calculations as dust when compared to this: To create life - in beauty?

What desire ye? What seek ye? Why work ye?

Is it not for life - in beauty.

Have ye forgotten that?

Then were your world a madhouse.

*

When the sun had gone down, the sea and the sky and the earth over where the mountains opened and the village lay began a dance of colour. Each yielded to the others' embrace. The brown mountain sank down among the plains through a sea of joyously glowing colour. Out along the horizon I was aware of a belt of green. How inviting the play of light in and among the red and blue clouds! I could glimpse no houses but I knew they were there. Smoke was rising from the little chimneys. I felt I could almost detect the smell of coffee as I looked at that shining patchwork of green.

And hill and field and sea merged together more and more and turned to dream. Who would believe that those soft deep-blue draperies yonder were made of rock as they ran down, soundless as tulle, to a sea that looked like a harp string gently vibrating between its beaches.

But see how from the folds of those blue fabrics there beckons a thin narrow veil. It grows longer and longer until finally it winds across the water like a violet ribbon along the breasts of the mountains.

It is the smoke from a steamer. A sign of people. And I am moved by a strong desire to be with those who are down there.

I want to go down to them, to hear them talking and laughing, all of them, hear them sing from the boats, see the flowers behind the curtains and stand listening to the muted playing of the piano in the twilight as they all sit together and dream.

Or if I could only find someone sitting alone and weeping who would allow me quietly to sit there and gently wipe away the tears.

Down to them, down to them, I whispered.

So I came down from the ice-fields to the people, and the fragrance increased, becoming fuller and more rounded, pine and birch, hazel and blossom and brook, and finally all things together: forest and gardens and roses and dew and mist and summer.

Draft Fragments

1. Oslo University Library, Ms.8⁰ 1424:26

On the evening of the next day I slipped in among the lights of the big city.

I wandered among the crowds, from street to street, from window to window. I wanted to see everything. Finally I stopped in front of a splendidly lit building. A gold-braided doorman carrying a marshal's baton stood at the entrance. It was the big and well-known dance hall. I went in. Doubtless my hand shook as I bought my ticket - priest, as I was. But I wanted to go in. I wanted to see all.

I had been tramping over the high mountains, past dark lakes and glaciers. For days I had looked upon the great wilderness. Suddenly here I was in the middle of a dazzling sea of light from a hundred electric lamps and candelabra.

Around me there was a swaying and a shaking. Everything was soft: the dresses, the steps and the rhythms of the dance. Couple close to couple, breast to breast. I watched these men and these women, saw rounded breasts circling and swaying, thousands and thousands of high-tilted breasts. I saw a thousand pairs of hips swinging and swaying. A thousand loins. Below the billowing skirts I saw the tiny feet tripping like flower stalks. Here again were those small black batons; the lines of the crystal, of rhythm itself. But those hips: how they undulated gently in elliptical paths like worlds. And those breasts: how they swung like twin moons around a common axis.

[In an earlier deleted draft, the above passage ran:

It was as if hundreds of planets had descended upon the earth and turned into blushing flesh and blood. I watched them as they swayed; in their feet I again saw that little black conductor's baton, and the rhythm - but those hips circled like worlds in elliptical paths and those breasts swung like twin planets about a common axis.]

There was no discord, no uproar. It was all a gliding and a swaying. The scent of the rhythms drifted away beneath those small twinkling toes, the melodies melted into the light, rhythmically rising and falling as the couples drew breath, rising and falling as the colour rose to their cheeks.

It could well have been that there was not a single rational thought there in the hall. But why should there be thoughts when thought itself had become flesh and blood and indeed more? Did they not live, did they not breathe, dance, sway? Were those thousand hips and thousand breasts not like the world itself as it danced - orbs of blushing flesh and blood? Were the men not like the axes about which they turned? Could any mathematician conceive a more splendid thought than this? And yet this was all much more even than mathematics, for there was soul in the air.

Look at those shining eyes! Look at the glances of the men, burning, setting breasts and hips aflame!

As I stood there, I could feel the currents, invisible. Within those bodies a throbbing urge was born of those rhythms, crept along the spine like a bowed violin string, moaned sweetly like the sound of a cello in those thousand breasts, rippled through those thousand hips, sweeping higher and ever higher in ever lovelier curves until fire entered into them, until those eyes no longer dared look into each other, until all was body and flesh, until axis and orbs became one in the darkness deep within those scented chambers.

Is there anything more beautiful?

The gleam in the dark eyes of the man who even now swings his woman past me sends forth a seed. It begins in music and in colours within which the women tightly clothe that beauty which is theirs so that it might shine resplendent.

[*In different mood, another manuscript fragment reads:*

There were women who lifted up their naked legs and the men clapped. All to a sweet melody. Women with soulless faces and hoarse voices.

I looked at the faces around me; and more and more a terrible image presented itself to me:

Syphilis!]

2. Moses rod: Oslo University Library Ms8⁰ 1424: 24

I got the pencil. They did not want to give it to me. I asked for pencil and paper. They said I was too sick. That I was not up to it. - I said I must, I must. I said it was the one thing that could give me peace.

Where am I? In a hospital. I am lying in bed. I think I have been sleeping for many days. I was in the arms of death.

I must make haste. What if my powers are not enough! I must write. I must tell. People must know.

What must they know? Do I know more than them?

The pencil shakes. But I must write. I must make haste. What have I written? What was it I said? Am I sick?

It was in church. Yes, now I remember. It was in church that it began.

*

Have I slept? Have I slept again? Who called to me? There is nobody here. The orderly has gone. Who called to me? Somebody said my name. I heard my name in my ear. I heard a sound. Like wings.

- Have I written that? What have I written? When did I write it?

Now I remember: it was this morning. I got paper and pencil. And now it is evening. The light is burning on the little table. Why does it not burn all night? Why have they not put in a little night-light? When I wake at night, I do not know where I am. I do not remember where I am. I *will* not lie in the dark at night. I *will* not. I *will* not see all those faces again. I *will* not.

How nice that they gave me pencil and paper. For I must write it down - I must make haste. Death is coming.

People must know. I must summon up all my strength. I must write it down. Perhaps I am the only one who can say it. I know nothing. My body burns. The words burn within me. It must not die with me. My brothers, the people, must know it all. •

What am I writing? Can they read it?

God wanted them to give me paper and pencil. He wanted me to write. Jehovah, Jehovah, where are you now? Where are you out in that vast space? Your vast space?

Has it been night since I last wrote? I must think things over. I must be calm. No, it was morning. I woke. I felt so strong, so powerful. I wanted to trumpet the spirit of the word throughout all the kingdoms of the earth. I asked for paper and pencil.

The word! The word that is carried from spirit to spirit - a little pencil - a rod fell down to Moses and he wrote - and it went from generation to generation - the word, the word.

'The word became God, and it was in us.'

I must be calm. I do not know what I write. I must tell things in sequence. I must not tell what is *mine*, but that which happened to me.

I am tired.

*

My head swims. It was something so great. Do I have any shred of that great thing within me that it might be passed on through me.

I begin to remember. It began - ah, I remember - I was a priest -*I* was a priest - *I* was to bless the others.

They sat below me, head upon head. Oh, those poor people! They came seeking help. They came to hear something from out there, from far out there, through me.

- I am calmer. Yes, I am calmer today. One can read what I write.

Did I sleep in the night? I heard glorious music as from a thousand great organs. A thousand mighty organs in the church of heaven. I once wrote - to think that I remember it, yes, I am calmer, I am calmer -I wrote that there ought to be great vast hymns for them to sing.

Yes, that is what people need. They should walk in massed ranks over the earth singing great vast hymns to the God of heaven, to the God of the sun, to the God of majesty, to the God of joy, to the God of peace!

Did I sleep in the night? I am so strong. I must surely have slept. Yes, I have. For I remember that I suddenly saw the sun. The sun that came in at the window. The sun that came into my heart. A ray of sunlight kills ten thousand fears. A ray of sunlight is more dangerous than the sharpest lance.

Yes, the light! For he is also called the light in the bible. Also the light.

- I do not write. I do not write what I *should* write.

Oh God, what is it that stabs at my heart. I am not strong enough. My head is often so weary. I must lay it on the pillow.

How good a pillow is! One lays one's head on it and all the world seems to grow silent.

Tomorrow I must begin.

SELECT BIBLIOGRAPHY OF WORKS IN ENGLISH

Sigbjørn Obstfelder, *Poems,* translated by P. Selmer, Norwegian and English, Sheldonian Series, no.6 (Oxford, 1920)

James McFarlane, 'Sigbjørn Obstfelder' in *Ibsen and the Temper of Norwegian Literature* (London: Oxford U.P., 1960), pp.104-13

Mary Kay Norseng: 'Obstfelder's Prose Poem in General and in Particular' in *Scandinavian Studies* 50 (1978) pp.177-85

Mary Kay Norseng: *Sigbjørn Obstfelder* (Boston: Twayne, 1982)

George C. Schoolfield, 'Sigbjørn Obstfelder: A Study of Idealism' in *Edda* 57 (1957) pp.193-223

SELECT BIBLIOGRAPHY OF WORKS IN ENGLISH